Blaze

Dear Reader,

What is it about a cowboy that appeals to so many women? Is it their pioneering spirit? Their quiet strength and determination? Or maybe John Wayne movies convinced us the cowboy represents honor and nobility. Of course, the rugged good looks of a man in snug worn jeans, cowboy boots and a Stetson sure don't hurt.

I live in rural Utah surrounded by a bunch of ranches. Mail isn't delivered out here. I have to go into town to pick it up once a week. Between the post office and the small market where I shop, I'm bound to see a cowboy or two. We might say hello to each other, or he'll give me a nod and I'll give him a smile. I honestly don't always remember a face—it's the cowboy image that lingers in my mind.

Nathan Landers, the hero in this book, is a rancher. He grew up on the family ranch and knew early on that ranching was what he wanted to do with his life. Unfortunately, his dogged pursuit of building his own place cost him a wife and potential family.

He's a damn good cowboy and businessman, no one would question that. But it's Beth Wilson who teaches him how to be a hero, and a man that a woman can depend on.

Best wishes!

Debbi Rawlins

Behind Closed Doors

—

Debbi Rawlins

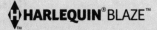

Recycling programs
for this product may
not exist in your area.

ISBN-13: 978-0-373-79816-2

BEHIND CLOSED DOORS

Copyright © 2014 by Debbi Quattrone

This edition published by arrangement with Harlequin Books S.A.

For questions and comments about the quality of this book, please contact us at CustomerService@Harlequin.com.

® and TM are trademarks of Harlequin Enterprises Limited or its corporate affiliates. Trademarks indicated with ® are registered in the United States Patent and Trademark Office, the Canadian Intellectual Property Office and in other countries.

Printed in U.S.A.

ABOUT THE AUTHOR

Debbi Rawlins grew up in the country with no fast-food drive-throughs or nearby neighbors, so one might think as a kid she'd be dazzled by the bright lights of the city, the allure of the unfamiliar. Not so. She loved Westerns in movies and books, and her first crush was on a cowboy—okay, he was an actor in the role of a cowboy, but she was only eleven, so it counts. It was in Houston, Texas, where she first started writing for Harlequin, and now, more than fifty books later, she has her own ranch...of sorts. Instead of horses, she has four dogs, five cats, a trio of goats and free-range cattle keeping her on her toes on a few acres in gorgeous rural Utah. And of course, the deer and elk are always welcome.

Books by Debbi Rawlins

HARLEQUIN BLAZE

491—TEXAS HEAT
509—TEXAS BLAZE
528—LONE STAR LOVER****
603—SECOND TIME LUCKY^
609—DELICIOUS DO-OVER^
632—EXTRA INNINGS
701—BAREFOOT BLUE JEAN NIGHT~
713—OWN THE NIGHT~
725—ON A SNOWY CHRISTMAS NIGHT~
736—YOU'RE STILL THE ONE~
744—NO ONE NEEDS TO KNOW~
753—FROM THIS MOMENT ON~
789—ALONE WITH YOU~
801—NEED YOU NOW~

****Stolen from Time
^Spring Break
~Made in Montana

With huge thanks to my editor, Laura Barth, a terrific team player who understands the big picture.

1

"WELL, YES, MR. JORGENSON," Bethany Wilson said as she kicked the stupid broken door propped up against the stupid wall. "Of course I'm upset. You gave—" she kicked it again, making sure her voice was modulated at a pleasant pitch "—away—" one more kick, hard enough to crack the center panel "—my lumber."

Her chin dropped to her chest when the older man went into his long monotone spiel again. Verbatim.

Amazing. Yet he couldn't remember that she'd placed her order first. The day before Nathan what's-his-name placed his. Though he was obviously a preferred customer at the local hardware store because he now had possession of her desperately needed order.

"When's the next shipment due?" she asked, cutting in.

His hesitation either meant bad news or he was miffed at the interruption. Or, more likely, he was distracted by one of his regular customers. Beth didn't even rank. Having moved to town only three months ago, she'd been relegated so far to the back of the line she might as well be sitting two states over.

"Let's see," he drawled in his slow, creaky voice. "I suppose I could get you something by Friday."

"Friday? As in four days from now?"

"I believe that's what I just said, young lady."

"Come on, Mr. Jorgenson. This is the second time I've had to wait for materials that you—"

"Keep your britches on, Clyde, I'll be with you in a minute." He was obviously holding the receiver away to speak to a customer. Probably wasn't even listening to her. "Now, what's that you were saying?"

Beth sighed. What was the point? Complaining wouldn't get him to move any quicker. Montana was beautiful this far north, but a bit isolated. If the hardware store's next delivery wasn't until the end of the week, there was nothing she could do about it. "Fine. Friday. If anything changes, please let me know."

"You betcha." His dentures clacked. "Have yourself a fine day."

Beth calmly disconnected the call, then dropped the phone on her makeshift plywood desk. That was the trouble with cell phones. You couldn't slam them. Pushing her fingers through her tangled hair, she winced at the tugs on her scalp. God, she used to be so good at getting people to do what she wanted.

Not here, though. Not in Blackfoot Falls.

She could run naked down Main Street and maybe make the headline of the *Salina Gazette*. Oh, she'd be juicy gossip fodder for weeks and have to suffer indignant glares from the women shopping at the Food Mart. But that would be it. The boardinghouse renovation would still be behind schedule, with workers not showing up, her lumber and other supply orders hijacked...

Maybe she was looking at the getting-naked angle all wrong. Maybe if she streaked through town she'd receive her shipments on time and workers would be lining up. But only if the men liked what they saw. She glanced down at her tummy. She'd been born and raised in Billings, Montana. And since returning to her home state she'd enjoyed homemade comfort food a little too much. In a fair world, stress would be eating away the extra pounds she'd gained. But no…her jeans had gotten tight.

Yep, lumber and drywall might be in short supply, but stress she had in abundance. Between her flaky sister and rebellious niece—for whom she'd moved to Blackfoot Falls—and working like crazy to turn the early-1900s boardinghouse into an inn, she was ready to pop like a damn cork.

At first, reconnecting with her family had been great, everything she'd hoped it would be after receiving the subtle plea for help from her estranged sister. Right before the not-so-subtle SOS text from her fifteen-year-old niece. Beth had been working in Europe at the time but she'd quickly wrapped things up and left her corporate job behind to be the loving aunt who would completely fix things between mother and daughter. Not play referee in a game no one could win.

"Knock, knock."

She looked up. Rachel McAllister stood in the open doorway. It was for her out-of-town wedding guests that Beth had promised to have the inn up and running by the first of February. No pressure.

"What brings you to the big city?" Beth jumped up to move the blueprints and notebooks off the spare folding chair.

"You don't have to get up," Rachel said as she entered the small room that Beth had sectioned off from the original kitchen. "I'm on my way to the market, but I figured I'd see if you had time for coffee."

"Sure. I have a pretty decent Colombian blend if you want to stay here. I can even make espresso." Beth gestured to the silver coffee station she'd ordered a day after she arrived and had one sip of Marge's weak brew. "Or we can hit the diner."

"Yeah, you like the really strong stuff. You must've gotten used to it while working in Europe."

"I did, but I don't mind going over to Marge's either."

"I wonder if she has any cinnamon rolls left," Rachel murmured.

"Um, no."

"You already checked?"

"I bought the last one." Beth tugged at her snug waistband. "Don't give me that look. I did you a favor."

Rachel grinned. "You're right. I need to fit into the wedding dress I ordered. Let's stay here."

Beth watched Rachel survey the stripped walls and the sizable holes left from heavy framed pictures that had hung for decades. She had to be worried about whether the place would be finished in time, but she didn't ask.

Until Beth had moved to town, she hadn't known Rachel.

Rachel's family owned the Sundance ranch, where they raised cattle. Recently they had converted unused space into guest quarters. She'd done a hell of a job cashing in on the popularity of dude ranches. Her success had motivated Beth to buy the boardinghouse and make it into an inn with a bed-and-breakfast feel. As long as her sister and niece lived here, Beth wasn't going anywhere, but she still needed something to do. Once she jumped the remodeling hurdle and got the place running, managing a small inn would suit her perfectly.

"Help yourself," she said, gesturing to the coffee and minifridge. "There's milk and cream. Sugar and sweeteners are in the silver tin."

"How's the work coming?" Rachel grabbed a mug.

"Did Mike Burnett give you a good bid for the finish carpentry?"

"He's putting one together now."

"I heard he's reasonable, especially considering he's the best carpenter around." Rachel fixed her coffee, then sat on the folding chair. "It's awfully quiet. Anyone working?"

Beth sighed. "The plumber's supposed to be here after lunch. I'll believe it when I see him. A lot of guys don't show up…they don't even call."

"It'll be better after hunting season," Rachel said. "But you're from Montana, so you know that."

"Actually, I'd forgotten how things slowed to a crawl this time of year. I'm glad you said something." She thought about the two guys who'd sworn they'd report early tomorrow. They'd mentioned something about not having tags, which now made sense. Evidently their names hadn't been drawn in the lottery designed to restrict the number of hunters for certain types of game.

"You were twenty when you left, right?"

Beth nodded. "It seems like a lifetime ago." She and Rachel had grown up in the same state, but any similarity ended there. Rachel had had the life Beth had always wanted. A home in the country, horses, a loving family. Definitely not living in a dusty trailer park with no parental supervision to speak of and a sister who was trouble from the word *go*.

"So everything else is going okay?"

Beth leaned back with a snort. And then it registered. "Hey…you probably know him…." She straightened. "Nathan—his last name starts with an *L*…"

"Landers?" Rachel frowned. "Nathan Landers? Sure, what about him?"

"Either Mr. Jorgenson got our orders mixed up or

Landers got pushy so Jorgensen decided to give him the lumber I was supposed to have delivered today."

"Hard to say. I don't think Nathan's the type to strong-arm anyone, but I really don't know him very well. He has a big ranch east of here. I've seen his foreman in town, but not Nathan. Since he lost his wife, he mostly keeps to himself."

A widower? Well, that was just peachy—here she was thinking about driving over to his place to find out just what was going on. It wasn't as if she planned on being mean, but she didn't want to come off as badgering some poor old man in mourning. "I swear his name sounds familiar, but I can't think of any reason it should."

"I can't either. Technically he lives in the next county. Though Blackfoot Falls is closer to him than Twin Creeks."

"You mean he doesn't even use the hardware store in his own town?"

Rachel laughed. "I'm sure there's another shipment arriving soon."

"Not till Friday. And I have two guys who promised me they'd be here tomorrow." Beth picked up a pen and drummed it on the plywood. "So, in your opinion, would it be worth it for me to have a little chat with Mr. Landers? Is he the reasonable sort?"

Rachel pushed her auburn hair back and narrowed her green eyes thoughtfully. "What did you have in mind?"

"Nothing crazy." Beth smiled. "Don't look so worried."

"Oh, I'm not worried," Rachel said, and come to think of it, she actually seemed a bit amused. So maybe Beth was the one who should be concerned. "I think it's worth a shot. He's probably just storing the lumber for winter jobs to keep his men busy."

Beth glanced at her watch. If he agreed to let her have the order, she'd have to pick it up herself. Her truck was small, but she could make two trips. And if she waited for Liberty to be done with school, she'd help. Her niece might whine, but too bad. The budding graffiti artist needed the extra money Beth paid her to cover court costs as part of her probation. Beth really hoped that particular bud had been nipped. "I'll give him a call."

"Better yet, drive out there. It'll be harder for him to say no face-to-face." Rachel smiled. "I can give you directions."

"Good." Beth would still call. She'd never cared for that business of just showing up on someone's doorstep uninvited. Though she'd end up at his ranch whether he said yes or no.

Nine years working all over the globe as a corporate meeting planner had taught Beth tact, grace and the art of persuasion. She'd be damned if Blackfoot Falls was going to teach her patience.

NATHAN LANDERS JOINED his foreman at the corral fence. "What do you think of him so far?"

"The kid's got grit, I'll tell ya that," Woody said, his gaze glued to the young man stroking the mare's neck.

"He get on her yet?"

"Twice, and ended up with a mouthful of dirt both times."

That didn't surprise Nathan. He'd known the horse wouldn't be easy when he bought her. She'd taken the bridle just fine, and the bit hadn't seemed to bother her. But she sure hadn't liked being saddled.

He watched Brian give the mare's neck a final stroke, then slowly fit his booted foot into the stirrup. With impressive grace, the kid swung into the saddle.

For a moment the mare just stood there, almost as if in shock that the fool had climbed on again. The second it wore off she burst into motion, rearing up on her back legs, then twisting and bucking. Nathan and Woody both moved back when the mare came close to the fence, trying to brush the kid off.

She bucked a few more times, then came down hard, lifting her hindquarters and sending Brian over her head. He hit the dirt in a cloud of dust and with a string of cusses. The kid was only eighteen, and easily sprang to his feet. The mare eyed him warily and shied to the other end of the corral.

Woody yanked off his hat and waved away the dust. "He ain't bashful about getting right back on."

Nathan nodded. He'd heard that Brian was good with animals, and he'd obviously already passed the test or Woody would've sent him on his way by now. "I'm assuming you want to hire him."

"Up to you, boss." Woody scratched his balding head, then slapped the battered tan Stetson back on.

Nathan just smiled. He might own the Lucky 7 but very little was up to him anymore. Woody Knudsen held the reins when it came to the cattle operation. Ever since Anne's death, Nathan had lost interest. He still kept abreast of what was going on, met with the accountant quarterly and signed the checks, but the daily stuff was all Woody's.

Now, the two Arabians that Nathan had recently purchased were a different story. He still had a lot to learn about breeding them, but at least the idea sparked some life inside him. Three years was a long time to feel nothing.

"Bad time to be hiring with winter coming, but I say we bring him on." Woody propped his arms on the fence while he watched Brian go another round with the stub-born mare. "You're gonna need help with those Arabians at some point. Might as well see what the kid's made of."

Nathan should've known this was about Woody look-ing out for him. Woody had worked on Nathan's parents' ranch as a wrangler and eventually the foreman. He'd been there for Nathan's first step and when he'd climbed onto his first horse. And when Nathan had returned from college full of determination and too much ego, dead set on turning his own meager seven acres into one of the largest ranches in northern Montana, Woody had never doubted him.

Much as Nathan loved his parents—good, salt-of-the-earth, hardworking people—he hadn't seen the faith in their eyes that he had in Woody's. Now, at the wiser age of thirty-four, Nathan understood they'd had reason to be skeptical. But that took nothing away from Woody's unwavering support.

"He might wanna start right away," Woody said. "Un-less you have a problem with that."

"Nope." Nathan used his sleeve to blot the sweat on his forehead, then readjusted his Stetson. October mornings and evenings were nice and cool, but the direct afternoon sun could still be sweltering some days.

"You expecting company?" Woody stared past him toward the driveway.

Only if hell had frozen over. Nathan turned and saw the small blue pickup. It was too far away to see who was driving, though it didn't matter. He hadn't invited any-one, and folks who knew him knew better than to show up without being asked.

A minute later he saw a woman behind the wheel wearing sunglasses, her blond hair pulled back in a po-nytail. She parked the truck close to the bunkhouse where the men kept their vehicles, then climbed out. Her legs were long, her jeans tight and she was wearing funny-looking boots.

"You know her?" Woody asked, squinting against the sun's glare.

Nathan shook his head, not that Woody noticed. He hadn't taken his eyes off the woman. Working in front of the east barn, Scotty and Justin stopped fueling the ATVs to watch her walk across the gravel. Even Big John pulled his head out from under the hood of the bale retriever. If that wasn't enough of a shock, since the guy had no use for women since his divorce, he grinned at her.

"Did you see that?" Woody muttered, brushing the dust off his shoulders when she veered toward them.

She wasn't dressed to call attention to herself, not in that oversize blue T-shirt, but she got it all the same. It was those legs. Damn, they were long. She had to be about five-nine, even without those silly boots. And she had just enough sway in her hips to fire up a man's pulse without letting him think he was being played. But a woman who looked like her? Who was used to men staring and not being bothered by it? Nathan had a feeling she knew what she was doing. Woody thought Nathan was cynical when it came to women, implied he was getting to be as bad as Big John. Nathan just hadn't forgotten how complicated they were.

"Hi," she said as she got closer, putting her hand out and smiling at Woody. "Mr. Landers? I'm Bethany Wilson."

"No, ma'am, I'm Woodrow Knudsen." He yanked off his hat. "You can call me Woody, same as everyone else."

Nathan folded his arms across his chest, though she hadn't even glanced at him. He'd finally realized who she was, right before she'd given her name.

Her smile stayed in place, and so did her extended hand. "Well, nice to meet you, Woody."

He dragged his palms down the front of his grungy Levis. "Ma'am, I'm awfully grimy."

"So am I." She pushed her sunglasses up on her head and inspected the dark smudges on her hand. "How rude of me not to have checked first. I'm sorry," she said with a soft laugh. "It's stain from yesterday, so it wouldn't have rubbed off on you. It doesn't seem to want to come off at all."

"Paint thinner ought to do the trick," Woody said, grinning so hard you could see where his back teeth were missing. He noticed Nathan watching him and sobered, clearing his throat. "This here is Nathan Landers."

"Oh." She turned to him and blinked, surprise flickering in her face. Her gaze went to his mouth and jaw, then slid up to his eyes. "I didn't—" She smiled again. "Mr. Landers, I'm Beth—"

"I heard you the first time." He kept his arms folded. "What is it that you want, Ms. Wilson?"

Her eyes narrowed, assessing him, her poise unshaken. "I left you two voice mails. I have the feeling you got them."

"I did."

"And had you wanted to talk to me, you would've returned my calls," she said very matter-of-factly.

"Sounds about right."

"What calls?" Woody asked, looking confused and peeved. "I thought you didn't know her."

He wasn't up to dealing with Woody's disapproval just because she was a woman. She hadn't been invited, period. "Go hire the kid," Nathan said, jerking his head toward the corral. "Let him start when he wants and pay him for today."

When Woody didn't move, Nathan frowned at him.

"First off," Woody said, jamming his hat back on his head. "I reckon I know how to handle a new hire. And second, I ain't gonna interrupt him in the middle of breaking that mare."

Beth had turned her gaze to the corral. It wasn't just her legs that had drawn his interest…she had pretty eyes, he'd give her that, too. They were kind of green with flecks of gold and brown. When she cringed and put a hand to her throat, he turned to see what had caused her alarm.

Brian had taken another trip over the mare's head and landed on his ass in the dirt. The kid cussed like a veteran. Woody chuckled and even Nathan smiled a little.

"Wow," Beth said. "Is this how you interview people? Good way to get free labor."

"What's that?" Woody obviously didn't understand her jab, but Nathan did, and he sure didn't appreciate it.

"Well, Ms. Wilson," he said, tugging down the rim of his Stetson to block the sun. "I'm sorry you made the drive out here for nothing. You should've taken the radio silence as a clue."

She stared at him, her lips parting. "Wait. Can't we talk about it?"

Nathan had started to turn for the house but stayed right where he was, his gaze lingering on her mouth. The shape and lushness of her lips went straight to the plus column, right under eyes and legs. A stiff breeze stirred stray wisps of fine blond hair around her flushed face and molded the T-shirt to her breasts. They weren't small. The damn plus column was getting too crowded.

"Talk about what?" Woody looked back and forth between them. "Hells bells, Nathan, do you know what this is about?"

"The lumber we had delivered this morning. Ms. Wilson seems to think there's a mix-up."

"Not exactly. Jorgenson gave you my shipment and he's making me wait for the next one. I know you've been a customer forever and I'm new to Blackfoot Falls, but it was wrong. He shouldn't have done that. I'm not implying it's your fault. Or your problem." She stopped for a quick breath. "I've had trouble getting workers, but I finally have two guys coming to my place tomorrow morning. But without the lumber..." She shrugged, her gaze flickering to Woody, then back to Nathan. "If you don't need it right now, or if there's any way you can wait until Friday..."

Her voice faded along with the hope in her eyes.

"Well, shoot, Jorgenson had no call to do something like that to such a pretty thing," Woody said, and boy, did she not like that comment.

Her shoulders went back, her lips thinned. Then she must've realized the old guy hadn't meant anything and she gave him a small smile. "It's bad business. And please, believe me, I know it's not your problem. I do. If you can't spare the lumber I'll get back in my truck and leave. You won't hear from me again."

They didn't need the order for a couple of months. Nathan knew it and so did Woody, who was glaring at him. And for no reason. No, he didn't like her showing up because he hadn't returned her calls. But he didn't like that Jorgenson had screwed her either.

And Nathan sure as hell didn't like watching her nibble that tempting lower lip and stare back at him. He didn't have time for this crap. He had business in the stables. "Go ahead, Woody, do whatever you think is best."

"That's for you to decide, Nathan," Woody said in an

ornery tone. "I got a new man to hire." He found another grin for Beth and even puffed out his chest some. "He'll do right by you, ma'am." He stopped midturn. "By the way," he added, his gruff voice gentled. "What you saw wasn't free labor. It was a test. Nathan won't hire a man who goes for a whip. Nice meeting you."

"Woody—"

Ignoring him, Woody hustled to the other side of the corral, his old bowlegs moving faster than Nathan would have thought possible.

He looked at Beth. Embarrassment stained her cheeks, making her eyes greener. She was still worrying that damn bottom lip.

"I'm so sorry. I was joking about the free labor. It wasn't funny," she murmured.

"Take the lumber."

"Thank you," she said, and caught his hand when all he'd meant to do was wave her toward the barn. She pressed her soft palm to his work-roughened one and shook. "Thank you so much."

She had some grip. He flexed his hand, trying to get her to let go. Touching her was a mistake. Man, did he not need this. Something was different about this woman. And deep down he knew…hell, he'd known even before he'd seen those long legs and sexy eyes that she was going to be trouble. The alarm bells had gone off the moment he'd heard her sweet, husky voice on his voice mail.

For three years he'd been fine, a certain part of his life had become manageable. And now she was making him think about sex. It wasn't just a small tug either. She'd cursed him with one of those itches that couldn't be taken care of in the shower. Right now what he wanted was down-and-dirty, hot, sweaty, honest-to-goodness, sheet-tangling sex.

That was why he needed her gone.

The sooner, the better.

2

"HEY, BETH."

She heard the familiar voice coming from behind. It was Craig, a guy she'd met at the Watering Hole, walking from the barn toward her. "Hey, yourself."

"What are you doing out here, darlin'?" He flashed her that boyish grin he used on every woman who entered the bar. "Looking for me?"

Beth laughed. "You caught me," she said, throwing in a coy smile. "Now, what was your name again?"

"Ouch." He was a couple years younger than her and liked laying on the cowboy charm, but he was harmless and knew how to take no for an answer. He slid his hat off when he reached her and wiped his smudged face with the red bandanna tied around his neck, his grin widening. "That's okay, darlin'. You know I like my women sassy."

"And I like my hired men working when they're on the clock," Nathan said, and how she could have forgotten he was there, even for a second, was ridiculous.

Craig didn't seem overly concerned with the gruff remark. "Wait till you hear that engine, boss. I got the tractor purring like a kitten."

Beth had turned to Nathan. She didn't think he was

really upset, but he was doing her a huge favor and she couldn't afford to aggravate him. She found him watching her, his whiskey-brown eyes taking inventory of her face and throat, and she felt that annoying flutter in her chest again.

He switched his attention to Craig, who'd asked him a question about the tractor, and this was the first chance Beth had to really look without fear of being caught staring. No ifs, ands or buts, she was going to kill Rachel. It didn't matter that Rachel was engaged. She still had a duty to warn a person about to meet a hottie like Nathan Landers for the first time. For heaven's sake, a simple heads-up was an unspoken rule that every woman understood.

The man was well over six feet of lean muscle with broad shoulders and a strong jaw shadowed by a day's worth of sexy dark stubble. His nearly black hair seemed to be cut in a traditional style, though he hadn't removed his hat so she didn't know for sure. And yes, she might've preferred it a bit longer but...

His gaze shifted back to her, those dreamy light brown eyes catching her off guard. "Where do you live?"

"Me?" She went blank for a moment. "Why?" she asked, noting the lazy, sensual curve to his mouth even when he wasn't smiling.

"Just wondering how you plan on moving that lumber."

"Oh. My truck."

He lifted the brim of his hat and frowned at her pickup. "That?"

She nodded. "Two trips ought to do it. I'm only going to Blackfoot Falls...to the old boardinghouse."

"You bought the place?"

"Yes," she said, sighing. "I'm turning it into an inn. Nothing elaborate, only a dozen rooms. I'm trying to keep the early-1900s feel to the place." She glanced toward the large single-level home with its beautiful stonework and arched entry. "The whole inn could probably fit in your house. It's amazing, by the way. I love all the details. Did you build it yourself?"

Their gazes met, the sudden distrust in his eyes taking her by surprise. He said nothing, his expression growing more aloof as he fished his phone out of his pocket.

So much for pleasantries. Fine. She was tired and already not looking forward to making a second trip. "Tell me where the lumber is and I'll move my truck."

"Inside the east barn," Nathan said absently, his attention on his phone as though he'd already dismissed her.

Miffed with his rudeness and trying not to react, she turned and saw several rust-colored buildings. The closest one was obviously a barn, and she guessed that the large, freshly painted structure behind it near the trees might be the stables. Everything, from the house with its wide circular drive to the dozen or so outbuildings, was in prime shape.

She cast another longing look at the lovely home with the oversize windows and rose beds.

It finally hit her.

How could she have been so insensitive? That home had to have been built for his late wife. Beth doubted he kept the gardens tended for his own enjoyment. Even the small charming courtyard between the wrought iron gate and the front door was well maintained.

"I know where the lumber is," Craig said, startling her because she thought he'd left. "I'll show you where to park, then go grab Troy. We'll have you loaded in no time."

"No." Beth shook her head. "Just point me in the right direction. I can handle the rest."

Craig snorted. "You can't load by yourself."

"You'd be surprised at what I can do." She smiled at his raised brows, leaving out that she'd bring Liberty on the second trip. "You're nice to offer, but I'm sure you have your own work to do. Where do I go?"

She didn't know if Nathan was still behind her or not, but that was where Craig's gaze went. With obvious reluctance, he motioned toward the building she'd pegged as the stable.

"Thanks," she said, and glanced over her shoulder. "And thank you, Mr. Landers. You've really saved my butt. Next time you're in town I owe you a beer."

His stunned expression was priceless. Though she hadn't meant to shock him. Or for him to actually look at said rear end. In fact, the beer offer had just slipped out. She'd only meant to impress on him that she was truly grateful.

She hurried toward her truck, ignoring the stares of the men working on an ATV engine, then briefly exchanged a smile with a dusty cowboy riding a chestnut past her. By the time she got behind the wheel, she was a little shaky from too much sun, adrenaline, or maybe too much Nathan Landers. Bad time to remember she hadn't replenished the water she normally kept in the pickup. At least she'd brought her work gloves.

Throwing the truck into Reverse, she started to back up, cringing when she ground the gears. This was the first manual shift she'd ever owned, but after three months she usually did pretty well. Of course she'd have to drive like a moron now, with a dozen men watching her. Nathan was probably having a chuckle. Though no reason for her to give a crap.

She still wished she hadn't mentioned the house, since it had seemed to upset him—but she had a feeling he was generally a grouch. A damn good-looking one. She darted a look in the rearview mirror.

He hadn't moved. Except he'd put away his phone and was focused completely on her. Arms crossed, of course, feet planted wide, an amused look on his handsome face. Well, wasn't she just tickled pink that she could provide him with a little afternoon entertainment.

She forced herself to concentrate on the gearshift and slipped into Drive. She wondered how much he was still grieving. According to Rachel, since his wife died he'd been sticking close to home. No mention had been made of what caused her death, though Beth doubted that mattered to a person in mourning. She'd never lost anyone close to her.

That wasn't entirely true. She'd suffered loss. Her mother wasn't dead, not as far as Beth knew, but for as long as Beth could remember, Paula Wilson had repeatedly disappeared into bottles of booze and the bed of any strange man who'd promised to take care of her.

Beth's older sister had followed a similar path, including getting pregnant at sixteen. Giving birth to beautiful baby Liberty hadn't been enough to straighten out Candace. Most nights she'd left the little girl with Beth. But when the toddler had started calling Beth "Mama," quick as a wink, Candace had latched on to no-good Lenny Ramsey, packed up Liberty and torn away the only person Beth had truly cared about.

And Beth's father? She'd never known him. Like any child she'd been curious about him at one point. But eventually she'd reasoned that if Paula had been attracted to him, and vice versa, he had to be a loser, so why bother searching? She honestly didn't even think about him. All that mattered to her now was reestablishing a bond with

Liberty. And Candace, too, though her sister didn't seem anxious to let go of her bad habits.

Beth spotted the three stacks of lumber just inside the barn and sighed. The order wasn't nearly enough for what she needed for the whole renovation, but more than she cared to load by herself. No complaints, though. If the workers showed up tomorrow, this would all be worth it.

After reversing the truck close to the lumber, she pulled on her bulky work gloves and got out. As she lowered the tailgate, she caught movement in her peripheral vision and turned to see Craig and another guy jogging toward her. Beyond them she could see Nathan Landers still rooted to the spot, facing them.

"We've got it, Beth," Craig said, lifting his hat and sweeping his long, dark blond hair off his forehead. "Why don't you wait over there on the chair by the fridge?" He motioned with his chin. "Get yourself something cold to drink."

"You want your boss to have a coronary? He's watching you."

"Nah, Nathan sent us over." Craig grinned. "I knew he wouldn't let you do this yourself. You know Troy?"

Tall and lanky, Troy looked younger than Craig. He immediately doffed his hat and mumbled a greeting.

"I've seen you playing pool at the bar, haven't I?" She smiled when his eyes widened in surprise, a pleased grin tugging at his mouth. The only reason she'd noticed him was because of his bright red hair, but she kept that to herself. "I really can handle this, you know," she said, picking up a board and transferring it to her truck.

Craig hefted five slats at once.

So did Troy.

Show-offs. She stood back and watched for a moment. They worked fast. She decided to go for broke and lifted three boards…and tried not to whimper. They weren't heavy, just unwieldy. She swung her load around and missed Troy's ear by a hair. And only because he had good reflexes.

"Oh, my God, I'm so sorry." She slid the boards onto the bed and spun around to Troy. Cupping his jaw with her hand, she searched his face. "Are you okay?"

"Yeah. Fine," he mumbled, blushing furiously.

"You sure?" she asked, inspecting his cheek. His skin was warm, probably because she was embarrassing him. But would he admit it if she'd grazed him?

"Um, Beth." Craig took her shoulders, turned her toward the back of the barn and gave her a gentle push. "Go sit. We'll do this faster without your help," he said, and started laughing.

"My balance was off," she protested, squirming away from him. "I can still—"

"You trying to maim my men, Bethany?"

Nathan's voice made her jump. And not just because it was deep and rich and warmed her from the inside out like a decadent sip of Rémy Martin. Very few people called her Bethany, and none of them said it like that.

She turned to find him standing in front of a maroon-colored truck with the Lucky 7 logo on the door. The pickup hadn't been there a few seconds ago. It was a really big extended-cab model you couldn't miss. The kind the towing company had used to repossess trailers in the park where she'd lived as a child.

"I'd appreciate you doing like Craig asked and stepping aside," he said to her, his mouth curved in a faint smile as he pulled on tan leather gloves. Then he dropped the tailgate. "Boys…lets load the Dodge first."

"Sure thing, boss," Craig said, and exchanged a puzzled look with Troy.

"Hold on." Beth had no intention of moving. "I don't want this to be a big production. Or infringe on anyone's time. I really am capable of doing this myself."

"I'm sure you are," Nathan said, and then ignored her and grabbed a whole stack of lumber. "You want to be useful? Grab me a bottle of water out of the fridge."

Well, didn't he sound like a man used to giving orders? She glanced at the other two who'd gotten very quiet, then reminded herself she wasn't in charge here. He could change his mind, renege on giving her the lumber and she'd be crying a river come tomorrow. On the upside, standing by and watching him move wasn't a bad deal. His rolled-up sleeves bared his corded forearms, and the light blue shirt was fitted enough that she could see the play of muscle across his back every time he hefted a load.

He stopped to adjust his Stetson and looked at her. "Do you know where the fridge is?"

Pressing her lips together to keep from making an unwise remark, she turned to Craig and Troy. "While I'm at it, would you like something?"

"No, thanks," Troy mumbled.

"Yeah." Craig flashed her a grin. "See if there's a beer."

She didn't see Nathan's expression, but she could imagine it wasn't pleasant seeing how Craig ducked his head and laughed.

"Just joking," he said, stopping to sweep his hair out of his eyes. "I'll follow you to town and get you unloaded. By then it'll be quitting time and I'll buy you a beer."

"I'll take care of Bethany," Nathan said, and, God, she had to stop letting his voice make her all gooey inside. "I have to go to the Food Mart anyway."

She nearly dropped the bottle she'd grabbed from

the ancient refrigerator. Catching the shocked looks on Craig's and Troy's faces, she knew her surprise was justified. Even if Rachel hadn't told her Nathan stayed away from town, Beth couldn't see him going to the Food Mart. He'd send someone else.

After he dropped that little bomb, the rest of the job was finished mostly in silence. She heard Craig quietly bet Troy twenty bucks that their boss didn't know where the Food Mart was located. Naturally Beth pretended she hadn't heard. The two guys were shooting her curious looks, probably thinking the same thing she was…that she might have something to do with Nathan Landers's sudden itch to go to town.

And, Lord, she hoped that was true. She got a little tingly just thinking about what it could mean. Long cool nights in Blackfoot Falls could use a pinch or two of something spicy. And he looked like a man who'd know just which ingredients to use.

"What now? You want the paint, too?"

She blinked at the gallon cans she'd been absently staring at—ten of them had been stored beside the lumber and now stood alone against the wall. She turned to Nathan and grinned. "You offering?"

His mouth curved in what could pass for a slight smile. "Thanks, boys," he said to Craig and Troy. "Go ahead and knock off early."

"You sure, boss?" Craig's face lit up. "Woody's gonna pitch a fit."

Nathan jerked a thumb over his shoulder.

The guys didn't have to be told twice. Quiet Troy let out a whoop and they both tore off toward the bunkhouse.

Beth shifted her weight from one foot to the other, suddenly feeling off balance now that they were alone. She needed to get in her truck and head back to town.

Give herself time to think. Her gaze drifted to the paint. "I've screwed up your project," she said, pulling off the gloves she'd ended up not needing. "Now you have paint but no lumber."

"One has nothing to do with the other." His gaze fell on her hands, and she wanted to childishly hide them behind her back.

Her nails were horrible, dirty and jagged. She hadn't had a manicure in ages. Not since she'd moved to Blackfoot Falls. "What should I call you?" she asked, and saw that she'd confused him. "And don't say boss. That won't fly."

There it was again…the almost smile. "Nathan." He took off his hat and ran his hand through his dark hair. "Craig calls you Beth. Is that what you prefer?"

She had to think about it. These days only her sister called her Bethany, probably out of habit. But Beth did love the way he said it. "Either one." She shrugged. "Beth is shorter."

Neither of them moved. They just looked at each other for a long silent moment that should've been uncomfortable but somehow felt natural. Standing this close, she could see that he was bigger than she'd first thought. Broader and taller…maybe more muscular, but she wouldn't know for sure until she saw him naked. If she ever saw him naked. Oh, she really hoped so.

She cleared her throat and took a step back. "Well, I guess we should head to town. I've taken up enough of your afternoon."

He blinked, then ran his gaze down the front of her shirt to her jeans. "Come with me," he said, and walked farther into the dim, cavernous barn without a backward glance, as if it hadn't occurred to him that she wouldn't follow.

A little nervous that the shadows seemed to gobble him up, Beth hesitated and glanced over her shoulder. Craig and Troy were long gone. "Were you waiting to get rid of the witnesses?"

The words were barely out of her mouth when light flooded the barn and she whipped her gaze back toward the spot where she'd last seen him. He stood partly under the steps to the hayloft, between a cabinet and a workbench, watching her with a look of amusement. "You must be from the city."

"I'm from Montana," she said, a tad defensive and hoping he didn't think she'd *really* been nervous. To prove she wasn't, she strolled toward him, casually glancing at the bales of hay stacked as high as her shoulders, at the assortment of tools hanging on the rough-hewn walls, and inhaling the scent of oiled leather becoming more pungent this far inside. And tried to ignore the acceleration of her pulse the closer she got to him.

"Where?"

"Outside of Billings."

He barely reacted yet still managed to communicate "case closed." Oh, but he was so wrong. He gave Billings too much credit. She'd seen more than half the world. As far as cities went, Billings was peanuts.

She stopped several feet away to watch him rummage through a drawer. Without looking up, he said. "You have to come closer."

"Why?"

Nathan glanced up then, amusement gleaming in his eyes. "What do you think I'm going to do to you?"

"I have no idea." In spite of her effort to play it cool, her laugh sounded nervous, so she gave it up. "Why do *you think* I was ready to bolt?"

He held up a large can of paint thinner. "The light's better over here."

"I knew it was something like that," she muttered, and saw the corner of his mouth twitch before she sneaked another peek at her stained hands and awful nails.

"Let's see."

She slowly exhaled, then placed her hand on his outstretched palm. Of all the things she might've anticipated, this scenario was so far down the list that… Oh, hell, it hadn't even made the cut. It wasn't so much about the touching…it was his unexpected gentleness that made the contact feel irrationally intimate.

"Do you give manicures, too?" she murmured, watching him use a clean rag to rub each stain off her hand.

Still focused on his task, he responded with a patient smile, making her feel like a flustered twelve-year-old girl who didn't know how to talk to boys yet. The way he was acting reminded her of the way she treated the guys she met at the Watering Hole. She joked around with them all the time, never taking any of them seriously when they tried to hit on her. They were all younger than her, and none of them were her type.

Oh, damn, payback was really gonna be a bitch. Nathan was the first man she'd met in Blackfoot Falls who appealed to her. She was twenty-nine and she guessed he was in his early thirties. Good age difference in her book, but maybe he simply wasn't interested. Maybe he didn't care for blondes or tall women. Maybe he was the sort of man who would never get over his dead wife.

"There you go, Bethany," he said, meeting her eyes, his gaze lingering. "The sink is over in the corner."

"Thanks." She did a prompt about-face so he wouldn't see her giddy smile and scooted off to wash her hands.

He'd done a thorough job of getting rid of every little mark.

She'd wager he was just as thorough in the bedroom, and holy crap, did she ever want to find out if she was right.

3

NATHAN WATCHED HER stop to stretch her back. Bethany had clearly waited until she thought he couldn't see her. Though she hadn't complained once, and even tried to increase the loads she carried from the truck to the front porch, he knew she wasn't used to this much manual labor. Twice he'd asked her to step aside and let him finish. Might as well reason with a mule.

If he'd known she was going to be so stubborn, he would've brought Craig with him. But Nathan hadn't been thinking about getting the job done quickly or efficiently when he'd offered to bring the lumber. The fact was, he hadn't thought much past those long legs and smoky hazel eyes.

"I changed my mind," he said when she returned for more boards. "I'll take some water." He hefted six slats onto his shoulder and caught her eyeing him with a suspicious frown.

"I saw a whole big bottle of water in your truck. Think I don't know you're trying to get rid of me?"

"You have some interesting paranoia issues you might want to get checked out." He lowered his load to the second stack they'd started and then reached for the two boards she'd snatched off the truck. "Your water is probably cold. Mine isn't."

She narrowed her gaze, staring him down and holding firm to her bundle…until his knuckles grazed her breast and she let go. He hadn't meant to touch her like that, but her startled reaction made him smile all the same. Luckily she didn't see because he'd already walked past her.

He set down the boards and shook his head at the pair of new dark green shutters. The loose white siding around them was in sorry shape. A good wind could carry off the weathered clapboards. "You do realize you'll have to take these shutters down again."

"Yes, I do." She pulled off a glove and scratched the tip of her nose. "To fix the walls and windows. And the new door will have to come off, too," she said, stepping back to admire the repairs. "That's okay. We won't get to the front for a while. The place can look nice in the meantime."

The right side of the porch had been reinforced, but the plank floor on the left was still sagging. At least the steps had been replaced. "You working mostly on the inside?" he asked.

"Yes, I know I should make the most of the good weather but I take whatever labor I can get when I can get it." She removed her second glove and stuffed them both between her clamped knees while she loosened her ponytail. A breeze played with her long wavy hair, the honey-colored strands getting away from her as she tried to secure them in one hand. She put her hair back in the ponytail, more tightly this time. "I'll admit, at first I hadn't considered the weather turning quickly. I've never tackled anything like this before."

The sound of someone gunning a neglected engine snapped him out of his trance. "You're a brave woman," he said, annoyed that he'd been staring when he should've been hauling lumber.

Pulling her gloves back on, she followed him to his truck. "Or stupid. Guess I'll know in a couple of months."

He threw a look at the tired white structure as he grabbed another load. "That might be too optimistic."

"I know." Bethany sighed. "I wouldn't care when it got done except I promised Rachel I'd have it completed in time for her wedding. She has friends who'll need accommodations."

"Rachel?" He stopped and thought for a second. "Little Rachel McAllister? She's getting married?"

Bethany laughed, and she didn't hold back. "Little? Are you sure you're thinking of the same Rachel I'm talking about?"

Nathan smiled. "I don't know her well. I went to school with her two older brothers until the eighth grade," he said, and caught her puzzled frown. "County-line dispute. When the dust settled, my brothers and I went to Twin Creeks High."

"That must've been awful for you."

He shrugged. "We already knew every kid within a hundred miles. And I got to play football without having to compete with the McAllister brothers. I wonder if those boys ever stopped growing."

She laughed again. "Cole might be taller than you, but I doubt Jesse or Trace is."

"I'm only six-two."

"Only?"

He watched her balance the pair of boards she'd grabbed, trying hard to keep his attention off her legs and butt. "You're pretty tall yourself."

She opened her mouth to say something, but then tilted her head to the side and looked past him toward the street.

"Nathan Landers? My word, is that really you?"

"Ah, Jesus," he muttered under his breath, though he didn't recognize the excited voice coming from behind him. This was the third time someone had slowed down to convey their heartfelt shock at seeing him. The boardinghouse was located at the edge of town, but right on Main Street. He should've known it would be a circus.

He turned and saw that it was the white-haired Lemon twins. One sat behind the wheel with a pinched frown aimed at the sister leaning across her and doing the talking. He couldn't remember either of their first names or tell them apart. What he did know was they probably shouldn't be driving, since the big old Chevy was taking up both lanes.

"Afternoon, ladies," he said, touching the brim of his Stetson and keeping an eye out for oncoming traffic.

"How long has it been since we've seen you in town, Nathan? Two years? Three? I see you're helping Beth. She's such a wonderful girl. Very considerate, and pretty to boot. Won't it be nice to have the old boardinghouse open again?"

"For heaven's sake, Mabel, give the man a chance to answer." The driver jerked her shoulder and shifted to face him, obviously trying to force her sister back to the passenger side.

"Miss Lemon?" He gestured to a black truck heading toward them.

Her eyes got wide and she fumbled for the column shift. "Darn it, Mabel. Give me some room before we have another accident."

Nathan winced. He saw she was growing more nervous and jerking on the stick. The car lurched to the rear. "I think you have it in Reverse," he said, releasing his load back into the bed and putting a warning hand up to the driver of the approaching truck. As soon as Nathan reached the sedan, he crouched to check the steering column through the open window.

Miss Lemon found Drive. The Chevy pitched forward, and he jumped back, stumbling out of the way. He sensed Bethany behind him. Felt her hands grip his shoulders.

"Oops." She slid her palms down both sides of his spine, trying to steady him. Then she ducked her head around his body, keeping an arm wrapped across his back, and said, "Go ahead, Miss Lemon, steer toward the right lane. You're doing fine." She gave him a brief glance. "You okay? All body parts accounted for?"

"I think so." He hadn't actually lost his balance, but he liked having her so close he could smell her floral-scented hair. Feel the warmth of her skin through his shirt. "Might have to take inventory, though."

Her gaze snapped back to him. She gave him a long look, then let out a laugh and lowered her arm. Stepping away, she watched the Lemon sisters inch down the street.

Already regretting the inventory crack, he couldn't tell if she'd decided the words were innocent or loaded with a message he wasn't sure he could deliver on. Playing with fire without a means to extinguish it was plain dumb, and he knew better. He had to get sex off his brain. What he needed to do was get his ass home and quit eyeing hers.

"Don't they have kids or grandchildren who could drive them around?" With a worried frown, Bethany was still looking after the car.

"I don't think either of them married, but I'm not sure. They're in their eighties, right around my grandmother's age. She knows them."

"Does she still drive?"

"Not for a while. But she lives on the ranch with my

parents and two brothers. Plenty of people around to take her wherever she wants to go."

"At the Lucky 7?"

"No." He noticed the increasing number of vehicles crowding Main Street and knew he was in for a lot more small talk if he didn't keep his head down. "On my parents' ranch," he said, moving away from the street. "About twenty miles from me."

"Wow, that's great having your family so close." She reached the truck ahead of him and picked up two boards. "Assuming you get along with them."

He wasn't sure how to respond to that, or if he even should. Today was full of surprises. He'd kept to himself and the Lucky 7 for so long, he'd forgotten how to be social. How to talk to a woman and not second-guess himself. He'd been joking about the McAllister boys. Like them, he'd been one of the popular kids, the quarterback who'd led his team to the state championship twice, the guy who could've had a date every night of the week if he'd wanted.

College would've been no different if he'd had the time to socialize. He'd played football only to keep his scholarship alive, but spent the rest of his free time working to make his dream a reality. From the day he'd turned thirteen he'd wanted his own ranch. And at seventeen he was so confident of what lay ahead he could've carved his future in stone. At least the part about the Lucky 7. And marrying Anne.

"Nathan?" Bethany had already taken her load to the porch, and she stood there looking at him with troubled eyes. "Sorry, if I said something wrong. I know family stuff can be tricky."

Not until three years ago.

Shaking his head, he forced a smile.

After the accident, the well-intended lies and hidden truths had come out in force. Even before the funeral, everything around him, including his relationship with his family, had started falling apart. He'd never felt so helpless in his whole life. But you couldn't fix a marriage once the other person was in the ground.

"Hey, you still want that water?"

He blinked at Bethany. She hadn't moved. Her smile was brighter but her eyes were even more troubled. Her hands were tightly clasped, her fingers entwined. Great, he'd dragged his black cloud with him.

When he noticed she was slightly up on her toes, he didn't have to pretend to smile. He'd seen earlier that she was one of those high-energy types who tended to rock back on the balls of her feet when she wasn't in motion. The complete opposite of Anne. Even he was more laid-back these days. He used to be full of ambition, hated that there weren't more hours in the day. Maybe his new interest in breeding Arabians would bring back some of that drive.

"Ice cold, if you have it," he said, glad to see relief pass across her face. "I bet you were a bouncer when you were a kid."

She backed up to her new green door, wrinkling her nose. "A bouncer?"

"Not that kind—"

"Oh." She snorted a laugh and tried to cover it up. "How did you know?" Abruptly she looked down at her feet. "I don't still do that."

He smiled but kept working. The sooner he transferred the lumber to her porch, the sooner he could get back to the Lucky 7. Sure, he'd admit it, he was enjoying Bethany's company. Even knowing this little thing brewing between them would end right here. He glanced at what was left on the truck bed. In about twenty minutes, to be exact.

Ten if he worked faster.

BETH COULDN'T DECIDE if she should be insulted, mad or confused. Or perhaps she should just feel grateful that she had her wood for tomorrow and quit being a crybaby because she hadn't expected Nathan to want to leave so quickly.

The whole time she watched him pull up the tailgate, jam it in place and yank off his gloves, she tried to think of a reason to make him stay. But she'd already asked him if he wanted a tour of the inside, which he'd declined. Then she'd offered to buy him a beer, which he'd also declined. She'd even suggested she whip them up something to eat since they'd both missed lunch. He'd declined that, too, which was for the best, now that she thought about it. As her niece had pointed out, Beth's cooking sucked the big one.

The thing was, it had taken her no time to get his water. Just two minutes. Okay, maybe four, but only because she'd wanted to check her hair and see if she could use a dusting of blush. She'd resisted putting on lip gloss. Too obvious.

She couldn't shake the feeling she'd said or done something wrong. Probably because he'd worked like a madman to get so much done in her short absence. Clearly he was anxious to leave. Admittedly, it had to be annoying to deal with all the nosy, intrusive questions from passersby, but she wasn't suggesting they stay outside.

When he started to turn, she lifted her gaze from his butt. She'd been staring at it, too busy thinking to really enjoy the muscular roundness, and that pissed her off.

He picked up the uncapped bottle of water he'd left on the bumper, tilted it to his mouth and drank.

She tracked a stray drop running down his chin and wondered what it said about her eleven-months-and-counting dry spell that she was seconds away from dragging him inside and seeing what else that mouth could do.

Of course, she knew he couldn't actually read her thoughts, but when he swung a sudden glance at her, her struggle not to squirm turned pretty epic.

"Well, all right, Cinderella," she said. "I know you're worried about the whole pumpkin threat, so don't let me keep you." God, sometimes she said the stupidest things when she was nervous. It wasn't enough he seemed eager to bolt—now she was giving him a push.

Except...

Nathan was staring back at her, quite intensely, and she hoped she wasn't kidding herself, but he didn't look so anxious anymore. Finally he broke eye contact to look down at her feet. "Before I go, I have to ask..."

With a resigned sigh, she followed his gaze to her short camo-patterned cowboy boots. Only they were pink and tan, camouflage objective be damned. "A birthday gift from my niece, so I feel obliged to wear them occasionally."

"Ah." Amusement eased the tension around his mouth. "You're a very good aunt."

"You have no idea," she murmured, and stopped right there, deciding to avoid the topic. She suspected her earlier reference to family had darkened his mood.

He took another gulp of water, then recapped the bottle. "Good luck tomorrow. I hope your guys show up."

"If they don't, I'll hunt them down."

He smiled, and she had the distinct feeling he wanted to say something, but he started toward the driver's door instead. So that was it? He was leaving? Wishing her luck was a goodbye?

"Nathan?"

He opened the door but stopped to look at her, his face blank.

"Thank you," she said, wondering if she should offer to shake his hand. Normally she would, but now it felt weird. "I mean it. You could've easily blown me off, but you didn't."

"No problem," he said, his gaze slipping away from her. "Just being neighborly."

"I wish I could do something for you in return." She focused on his chin, horrified by the dip in her voice. It sounded huskier than normal, kind of sexy, kind of as if she was offering sex. She wouldn't mind a little harmless recreation, but being obvious wasn't her style. "So..." She cleared her throat. "If you're ever in town and feel like a beer, remember, I'm buying."

"I'll keep that in mind." His voice had lowered, too, and though she hadn't met his eyes, she felt him staring at her.

"That includes Woody, too. And Craig and Troy, of course. Please tell them." She saw a brief smile tug at his mouth and slowly lifted her lashes.

At that exact moment he turned away to toss his gloves onto the seat. "You don't owe them anything. They were being paid."

"Guess it'll be just you and me, then." She shrugged, which he missed, along with her teasing grin. So she was back to feeling awkward again. "Or not," she said, repeating the shrug when he looked at her before falling back a step. "Better hit it before the Food Mart gets crowded."

He looked momentarily confused and then tightened his mouth. Without another word he got into his truck.

She waited until she heard the engine start and saw the pickup roll forward before she turned to go inside.

If she were to glance back, she wondered if she'd find him watching her. Probably not. She might've only imagined the spark between them, but she didn't think so. Maybe he was still in mourning and wasn't ready to get back in the dating saddle. Had the tension between them made him feel guilty?

She couldn't stand it. She had to sneak a final look.

He'd just made the turn onto Main Street. And now drove in the opposite direction of the Food Mart, toward the highway leading back to the Lucky 7. Proof of what she'd already known. He'd used the store as an excuse. It pleased her and made her laugh.

"What was *he* doing here?"

The snarl in Liberty's voice had Beth jerking around to stare at her niece. She was coming from the stop where the school bus dropped off town kids. Candace and Liberty didn't live nearby, but she got off in town on the days she worked for Beth—who'd somehow managed to forget today was one of those days.

"Who?" Beth followed the spiteful gaze aimed at Nathan's truck. "Nathan Landers?"

"Yeah." Liberty gave a surly huff. "What the hell did he want?"

"How do you know—? Oh, God." Beth finally realized why his name had sounded familiar. She'd seen it on the victims' restitution list, the one that had been issued by the court. Nathan was one of the dubiously proud owners of Liberty's wall art.

4

BETH SAT AT the kitchen table, sipping her morning coffee as she listened to her sister and niece get into yet another argument. They were down the hall, probably in Liberty's room, but their rented house was tiny and Beth could hear every heated word.

This time the disagreement centered on how Liberty was dressed for school. A rather popular theme for them—although the shouting could've been about anything, ranging from using each other's things without permission to whether Liberty could visit her father in prison. Their differences seemed endless, and Beth felt awful for both of them.

Sadly, their quarrels weren't the typical mother-daughter stuff because Candace hadn't grown up yet. They sounded more like teenage sisters. At times Beth felt pathetically grateful she'd been spared ten years of the ongoing drama, but mostly she felt guilty.

Yes, she'd been only seventeen when her sister had taken Liberty and fled without even leaving a note. But contact had been reestablished five years ago, and Beth, wrapped up in her career, had ignored the signs they were headed for trouble. Turning a blind eye had been easy to rationalize. After all, she'd already done her share. At age eleven she'd started taking care of Candace and their mother, and then later Liberty, making sure they all had a roof over their heads and food in the fridge.

"Stop it, Candace." Liberty stormed into the kitchen, her long brown hair flying everywhere. She dropped her backpack on a chair and flung open the fridge. "You try to act and dress like you're still young, but you're not. You're old and you don't know what you're talking about. Girls don't wear that kind of shit to school anymore."

"Come on, Lib," Beth said quietly. Normally she didn't interfere, but she knew Candace wouldn't correct her daughter's language. "I know you have a better vocabulary than that."

The teenager rolled her eyes, but she'd watch her mouth…at least as long as Beth was present. They'd had a few discussions about showing respect.

"That's right. Listen to your aunt but ignore me." Candace swept a contemptuous gaze over Liberty's baggy jeans, oversize T-shirt and combat boots. "But she doesn't have a man, now, does she? And neither will you if you keep dressing like a damn slob." Candace shook back her overprocessed, bleached hair. "Old, my ass. Last week at that silly PTA meeting, I could've had any man I wanted. You shoulda seen them eyeballing me, even with their pig-faced judgmental wives sitting next to them."

"Oh, God, Candace, you're so pathetic," Liberty said through gritted teeth. She slammed the fridge door without taking out anything for breakfast. "Don't go to my school anymore. For meetings…for anything. Ever. I mean it."

Candace blinked and cast a nervous glance at Beth before reaching into the pocket of her black silk robe. Her cigarettes were never far.

Beth stared into her cup, using every ounce of her control to keep her mouth shut. For now. Just until Liberty left to catch the bus. Then she'd speak with her sister. For all the good it would do. Sometimes Beth wanted to just choke her and other times she could sob for hours. Candace had become a replica of their mother, abusing booze, ready to screw any man who paid her a compliment.

She was only thirty-two, but hard living had taken its toll on her skin and body. Beth held out little hope she'd change her ways, but she had to make Candace understand that her fifteen-year-old daughter was too young to be trying to attract a man. Or that she needed one to make her happy.

"Tell you what, Mom..." Liberty drawled, grabbing a handful of hard candy from the plastic bowl on the blue Formica counter.

Ah, here came the bargaining part. Beth had to admit, Liberty was pretty good at it. Or, more accurately, she knew how to wear her mother down.

Candace drew on her cigarette and grimaced. She must've forgotten it wasn't lit yet. Beth had convinced her to only smoke outside. Pulling the cigarette out of her mouth, she glared at Liberty. "What?"

The girl drew in a deep breath. She didn't look cocky or combative, but oddly nervous. "Let me see Dad next visiting day and I'll change into anything you want," she said, looking into her mother's eyes, an unconscious yearning in her youthful face. "I'll even wear some of that stupid makeup you bought me."

Clearly startled, Candace turned to the window over the sink. "I think I see your bus. You're going to be late, so move it."

"Oh. My. God. You're such a liar. You've been saying *maybe* for months." The words shook with anger. "You're never going to let me see him." Liberty grabbed her backpack. "I hate you." She nearly tore the screen door off its hinges and slammed it behind her.

Candace hadn't turned around once.

Beth got up and ran outside. Liberty had made it halfway to the short gravel road shared by three other shabby houses with their neglected yards. "Liberty, wait."

The girl hitched the sagging backpack up to her shoulder, looking small and forlorn standing in the middle of the weed-infested grass. After swiping at her cheeks, she turned and waited for Beth.

"I hate Candace," she murmured. "I do. I really hate her. Why couldn't you have been my mother?"

Beth hugged the girl. "No, you don't. I understand why you think you might." She drew back to smile at her niece. "When I was your age I hated my mother, too."

"Well, yeah, grandma and my mom are totally alike."

The teen's insight startled Beth. Maybe the right thing would be to deny it, but somehow that felt like an insult to Liberty. "You don't hate her," she said. "You may not agree with her, or like some things she says and does, but—"

"Do you think she's right? About not letting me see my dad?"

"I'm sure she has a good reason," Beth said carefully. "I don't know the specifics, and it is a four-hour bus ride to the prison."

"So what? I haven't seen my dad in a whole year. And it's not like I'm asking her to take me." Liberty briefly turned at the sound of the noisy bus still a mile down the road. "I'm old enough to go by myself."

No way Beth agreed with that, but she'd let it slide for now. "Let's walk to the curb so the driver sees you."

"Will you talk to her, Aunt Beth?" Liberty tugged the

overstuffed backpack up higher on her shoulder as she swung toward the road. A notebook popped out. And so did a can of red spray paint.

"Liberty." Beth sighed, feeling heartsick. She'd honestly thought they'd turned a corner. "What are you doing with that?"

"It's not what you think."

"What I think doesn't matter. Having spray paint in your possession violates your probation. The judge can stick you in juvenile detention."

"Oh, he won't." Liberty crammed everything back into her backpack. "Spike says the court always threatens stuff like that but they never lock kids up. It costs too much."

Beth really had to bite her tongue. If she had her way, Jerry Long, aka Spike, would be thrown in a dungeon somewhere north of the Arctic Circle. The guy was crude, surly and, at eighteen, too old to be hanging around a fifteen-year-old girl. "He's wrong, kiddo, and I don't want to see you get hurt." She held out her hand. "You need to give me that can."

"No, it's for a school project. My art class." Liberty sent a quick look at the approaching bus. "I don't want to have to explain to my teacher why I can't have a stupid spray can."

"What kind of project is it?"

"Please, Aunt Beth," she pleaded with puppy-dog eyes as she moved toward the road. "I'll give you the can as soon as I'm finished with it. Promise."

The bus stopped and the door whooshed open.

Beth sighed. "Okay. Go." She hoped she wasn't being foolish. "We're going to talk more about this later," she called after Liberty, who wasted no time getting on the bus and out of earshot.

The air was chilly and scented with the crisp smell of autumn. Wearing short-sleeved T-shirts was fine during the day, especially to work around the boardinghouse, but she'd have to buy some sweatshirts for the mornings. Goose bumps covered her arms and she rubbed them, trying to get warm, as she stood in the tall grass, watching the bus turn onto the highway.

How different her life was these days. She hadn't even owned a T-shirt until two months ago. Armani suits and Dolce & Gabbana dresses had hung in her closet. And her collection of shoes? Just thinking about her Jimmy Choos and Christian Louboutins languishing in a storage unit gave her another chill.

She stared down at her ugly work boots. God, she really missed high heels—mostly because she liked the way they made her legs look. But that was stupid, since all she ever wore anymore was jeans. Even once the inn was open for business, her attire wouldn't change much. Around Blackfoot Falls people only dressed up for church, weddings and funerals. And for some, that simply meant a clean shirt or wearing something other than jeans.

When she'd made the decision to quit her job and move close to Candace and Liberty, she hadn't considered the little things that would change in her day-to-day life. Her decision had been both emotional and hasty, but this was still the right choice. Although she wasn't anyone's idea of a perfect role model, her influence might be Liberty's only shot at a healthy future.

She turned and started back toward the small turquoise house with its peeling white trim. What an eyesore. Which really said something, considering the condition of the other three homes with their torn screens and ramshackle porches. She couldn't wait until a room was ready at the boardinghouse. Nathan was right—her efforts should be concentrated on fixing the outside, especially with winter coming. But she needed her own space. She needed to be away from this sad little neighborhood that reminded her of her unstable childhood.

Her aversion had nothing to do with being a snob. While working as an event planner, the fat paychecks had been well earned, not handed to her just for being pretty. She'd gotten her hands dirty plenty of times, making sure every event went smoothly. As much as she loved her designer shoes, she hadn't forgotten how often she'd had to literally run around, bribing and cajoling, fixing last-minute snafus and liberally cursing both Mr. Choo and Mr. Louboutin.

No, the real problem with living here was that it pushed her buttons. Thrust her back in time to feeling like that scared, helpless child, convinced she'd never be safe, never know the security of a home that couldn't be pulled out from under her. As clear as it was that she'd made the right choice to move to Blackfoot Falls, she was equally certain that she couldn't live in this house much longer. Beth needed her own space.

And the other unsettling thing? She suspected the rent was being paid by one of her sister's lovers. Or maybe the guy owned the house and was taking payment in trade. When Beth had offered to cover the rent and utility bills, Candace had eagerly requested cash instead of a check made out to the mysterious landlord. Beth had bought Liberty school clothes and a computer instead.

Candace was standing at the open door puffing on her cigarette. "I told you before you came that girl was a handful," she said, the corners of her mouth curling up as if the warning gave her reason to be smug.

"Is it any wonder?" Beth pushed past her. "She doesn't have adequate parental supervision."

Candace put the cigarette out on the side of the house and joined Beth in the kitchen. "You talking about me or her father?"

"Oh, God, really?"

"Hey, at least I'm here. I didn't get myself locked up for breaking and entering."

Beth sighed. "She shouldn't be hanging around Spike. He's too old for her."

"I agree. I even had a sit-down with Liberty."

Beth had picked up the keys she'd left on the table, but surprised, she was no longer in a hurry to go. "And?"

"I told her to wake up, that she's wasting her time. He's eighteen and still a junior in high school. She doesn't need a loser like him. He's never gonna be able to buy her something nice or take her anywhere. I told her straight up. I said, baby girl, you can do so much better than that clown."

Her mouth hanging open, Beth stared at her sister. The woman was completely clueless. Even after all the heart-to-heart talks they'd had in the past two months.

Candace took the tomato juice out of the fridge and fixed herself a Bloody Mary. After taking a sip, she glanced at Beth. "You want one before you go?"

Instead of answering, she saved her energy to keep from exploding. "Liberty is a bright girl. She doesn't need a man buying her things or—" Beth's control slipped a notch. "Or paying her rent."

With a chilly glare, Candace picked up her drink, leaving everything else on the counter, and walked to the door while reaching into her pocket.

"Look, I'm sorry." Beth briefly closed her eyes. "I'm not here to judge you, I'm not…but come on, this is about

Liberty. You don't want to see her go down the same road as—"

"Me?" Candace paused to look at her and shrugged. "Go ahead and say it."

"I mostly blame Mom, not you. She was a horrible influence on both of us." Beth had to be careful to keep her voice neutral. No one appreciated condescension, and she wanted to provide motivation, not ammunition for another fight. "The example you set for Liberty matters."

"Oh, for God's sake, Bethany, kinda late for that, don't you think?"

"No. No, I don't."

"Well, that's your job, isn't it, Little Miss Perfect? Being the shining example for your niece," Candace said, and slammed out the screen door.

Holding on to her temper by her fingernails, Beth followed her to the stoop. "Look, you called me, remember?"

Candace lit her cigarette and drew in deeply. "You heard from her recently?"

"Who?"

"Mom."

Beth shook her head. Candace's mercurial moods alone drove her crazy. "I haven't talked to her in two years. She could've changed her number or moved for all I know."

"I'm pretty sure she's still living with Bobby in Vegas," Candace said, absently staring off toward the Belt Mountains where most of the aspens had turned golden. The only decent thing about the house and flat tract of land was the view.

"Can we get back to Liberty? I think Spike is the one getting her into trouble."

"As long as he's not chasing off other boys who are interested in her, I'm not going to interfere."

Watching her gulp down half her drink, Beth sighed. Once again, it wasn't the time to have a worthwhile discussion. But then it never was with Candace. Beth glanced at the clock. She had to get to town and be at the boardinghouse before her workers arrived.

Thinking about them reminded her of the lumber order, which led her to Nathan. Yesterday he'd been a shining beacon of hope that life in Blackfoot Falls might be looking up. That had lasted for an hour. After he figured out she was related to the little graffiti artist who'd defaced his water sheds, he'd probably never want to see Beth again.

Not bothering to say anything to her sister, Beth left through the living room, grabbing her phone and wallet off the teak end table. The garage-sale purchase was the nicest piece of furniture in the house and even made the green plaid couch look better. As far as the brown corduroy recliner went, Beth saw no hope for it. Maybe she'd get lucky again at another garage sale.

She climbed into her truck just as her phone buzzed. She smiled when she saw it was a text from Fritz. He sent the same one every week, asking if she'd had enough and was ready to return to work. Her former boss had never said, but she had a feeling he hadn't expected her to last this long. He'd been good to her, grooming her to be a savvy, confident woman, and she owed him. It was time to make him understand he should hire another assistant.

Wondering where he was, her fingers hovered over the keypad. He could be in Paris or Hong Kong or New York. It didn't matter since he'd just texted. She wouldn't be disturbing him. Allowing herself a brief wistful memory of autumn in Paris, she stared at the sad three-bedroom house that was in desperate need of a new roof. She really had to move out. It wasn't that she needed pretty things. Arguing with Candace and getting nowhere was sucking the soul out of her. Still, she was committed to staying in Blackfoot Falls. Liberty needed her and, to some degree, so did Candace.

Beth dropped the phone on the seat beside her and turned the key in the ignition. She would have that talk with Fritz. Absolutely, she would. Just not right now.

5

NATHAN LEFT HIS office through the French doors that opened to the garden. He didn't know why he hadn't taken his normal route through the house and out the kitchen. It felt odd following the flagstone path. Generally he forgot the flower beds and whimsical-shaped shrubs were there.

Anne had designed the garden and wanted the impractical French doors so they'd match the other three in the den, living room and master bedroom. If she'd been disappointed that he tended to keep the drapes closed, she hadn't mentioned it and he hadn't noticed. But apparently, a lot of things in their marriage had gone unnoticed.

If he'd had his way, his office would've had a view of the stables and the grassy field that turned to pasture before climbing the foothills. It was all there, beyond the privacy hedge that prevented him from seeing anything but blue sky and the Rockies in the distance. But Anne had asked for so little.

Every now and again he considered cutting down the hedges, but hadn't followed through. He'd just left them, the way he had the roses. The gesture was a tribute to her, he supposed, though it was Kitty who took care of the flowers, along with the house. They'd hired her to help with the housework a year after he and Anne had married, and she'd been coming twice a week ever since. The woman had adored Anne. And he reckoned Kitty was fond of him, too, but if he ever got serious about getting rid of the garden she'd probably serve him his balls for breakfast.

Woody was leading the new mare toward the east corral when Nathan walked out from between the hedges. Big John and Troy were loading fence posts onto one of the trucks, and all three men did double takes. Hell, it wasn't that big a deal. A man had a right to walk through his own garden.

He cringed…even the thought sounded weird. Hoping to avoid Woody's meddlesome observations, Nathan veered toward the stables.

If he heard Beth's name one more time, Nathan was going to gag the old man. Better yet, call his bluff and force him to go on the vacation he'd been threatening to take for eight years. The minute Nathan had returned from town yesterday, Woody had started with the questions and making noises about it being time Nathan got back in the saddle before certain body parts stopped working. It would've been funny if the old man wasn't serious.

Even if Nathan was considering dipping his toe in the water, Bethany wasn't the woman for him. Not for the long haul anyway. She was pretty and outgoing, but she wouldn't last long in Blackfoot Falls. He'd bet she'd bought the old boardinghouse on a whim and hadn't given enough thought to the renovation. She should've been going full speed, getting the outside work finished before the first snow, then moving to the inside on wintry days. And not installing new shutters that would have to come down again, just to make the place look nice. That dilapidated old building needed a lot more than shutters to look anywhere near decent.

She had a lot of energy and enthusiasm, he'd give her that. And looking at the glass as half-full wasn't a bad attitude. That same sort of optimism had helped him get the Lucky 7 off the ground. But it only worked with a healthy dose of common sense. No, Bethany wasn't the type for him. He'd already had one idealistic woman in his life, and that had ended tragically. For everyone.

Nearing the stable, he saw Craig brushing Romeo outside the tack room up front. Anne had named the stallion. He was a handsome chestnut, and the lousy name had stuck in Nathan's craw, but again he'd allowed her that small win.

He never made decisions—especially ones that mattered—based solely on emotions. He didn't understand whimsical thinking. Maybe that was why he hadn't known his own wife. Though she'd apparently understood him well enough to hide certain things from him. Fanciful things. Like her dreams of being on the stage, in the spotlight. She knew he would've been confused or assumed she was joking. He might've blamed her friend Bella for filling Anne's head with nonsense and dragging her to those crazy auditions. But it was more likely that he'd have dismissed the whole thing.

He just wished he'd had a clue. Then maybe Anne wouldn't have ended up on the highway headed for Kalispell that night. Maybe she wouldn't have died.

Craig looked up from brushing Romeo, but Nathan wasn't in the mood to talk so he skirted the stables and kept walking toward the equipment shed.

Dammit, he didn't need all this crap surfacing again. He'd rehashed everything a thousand times already. He would never know how their lives might've turned out if they'd been more honest with each other. If he'd realized she had a dream of her own. One that hadn't necessarily included him.

If he wanted to feel guilty, he had plenty of other reasons. The strained ties with his family were all on him. He'd shut everyone out. The worst part was, he'd isolated himself for so long he wasn't having an easy time letting people back in. Not even his brothers. And Clint and Seth had always been his best friends.

Yet spending time with Bethany had been surprisingly easy. If she knew anything about him, or about Anne, which wasn't farfetched in a place like Blackfoot Falls, Bethany hadn't let on. Yesterday had felt like a clean slate. Just two people who were attracted to each other having a little fun.

He knew she'd felt the same physical pull. He'd seen it in those sexy hazel eyes. What he didn't know was whether the burning need for release had kept her awake last night, too. He'd taken care of himself once in the shower and then later in bed so he could finally get some shut-eye.

His venture into breeding Arabians had taken him out of town twice last month. He'd had the opportunity to hook up. He'd refrained, mostly because he wasn't ready. But it reminded him that he'd become the subject of rumor and uncharitable gossip after Anne had died, which was yet another reason Bethany wasn't right for him, whether she stayed or not. All he wanted was sex with no strings, period. If last names weren't involved, all the better. He'd grown up loving his small town, but that love had vanished with the truth about Anne.

That left Bethany out. And yet, something about her drew him like a bear to honey.

He'd honestly thought that, after some sleep and distance, the feeling would go away. He wished to hell he'd been right.

"NATHAN? IT'S BETH. Beth Wilson." She plugged her free ear and hurried out of her office so she could hear. Of course, the hammering on the other side of the wall had started the second she'd made the call. "We met yesterday."

"I remember," he drawled in a mildly mocking tone. "What can I do for you *now?* You need nails? Hammers? Lunch?"

She grinned. "Really? Lunch? Dinner would be better so I wouldn't have to come back to work, but sure, I'll go to lunch." At the expected silence, she pressed her lips together to keep from laughing. Until she couldn't hold it anymore. "Relax, I know you were being sarcastic."

He sighed, then after another pause, he asked, "Have you eaten?"

It was her turn to be shocked speechless. Her heart did a little two-step before she got it. Okay, he was teasing her back. Evidently he hadn't made the connection between her and Liberty. But Beth wasn't out of the woods yet. "Seriously, I do have a question. I'm horrified that I didn't bring it up yesterday, but how do you want to handle payment for the lumber?"

"I thought we were doing a swap?"

"We can." She glanced over her shoulder when the hammering grew louder, then took the porch steps and planted herself on the grassy area under the elm. "I've already paid Mr. Jorgenson, so that works for me. But if you have another order coming in Friday, I didn't want the accounting to get complicated."

She held her breath, hoping he'd take her explanation

at face value. Even with all the craziness the day had hurled at her, she couldn't stop thinking about yesterday. About him. About the possibility of them getting together. So she'd called to hear his voice, see if there was anything between them worth salvaging before she got ahead of herself. Before the subject of Liberty came up.

So far so good. Beth had teased him, he'd teased her back, so maybe…

"Since you've already paid him, I'll let Jorgenson figure it out. I trust him."

"Sure. He likes *you*."

Nathan's gravelly chuckle made her skin prickle. "Still paranoid."

"I just don't like having my hands tied."

"No?"

The deepening of his voice made the word sound suggestive. Okay, this was promising. If only she could think of a quick comeback…dammit.

"Your workers showed up," he said, his tone shifting back to normal. "That has to be a relief."

"You can still hear them hammering?" It was probably her heart.

"Nope. Not now."

"I think I'll have them for the rest of the week. Unless one of them stubs his toe."

"And here I thought you were the glass-half-full type."

Sighing, she leaned against the huge ancient tree trunk, thumping her head back a couple of times. "I shouldn't have said that. I'm not usually such a grouch. It's been a really bad day. Bad week. And it just started." She straightened. "Except for you. You were terrific yesterday." Grinning, she said, "I bet you're still terrific today, too."

Nathan barked a short laugh. "You setting me up?"

"For?"

"I don't know. I've got the feeling you want to talk me out of something else."

"Um…" *His jeans maybe,* she thought, and felt heat flood her face. "No," she murmured, more to herself. "No, I'm going to let that one go."

"Yeah." He quietly cleared his throat, and then she heard someone muttering in the background. "Sorry," he said. "They need me outside."

"Is this the best number to call?" she asked quickly. It was his landline, and she was hoping for his cell number. "You know, in case I think of something."

"To talk me out of?"

"Maybe."

"Hold on a second." It sounded as if he'd pulled the phone away from his mouth when he said, "I'll meet you outside in a minute, Woody." More muttering. "I'm back. Let me give you my cell number. Do you have something to write with?"

"I have a good memory."

"I'll keep that in mind," he said, and recited the number. "The one I have…is that your cell?"

"It is. Sorry I kept you." She saw the school bus pull away from the stop two blocks down but couldn't see Liberty.

"No problem." He hesitated. "I'll call later."

A shiver of pure pleasure slipped down Beth's spine. "I look forward to it," she murmured, then disconnected before her excitement tripped her up.

She spotted the trio of older girls who always got off the bus with Liberty and watched them disappear into the variety store. With them out of the way, there was still no sign of her niece. Beth pushed off the tree and craned her neck. Maybe Liberty had already ducked into the store for a soda.

"Hey, Beth…"

She glanced at Larry, who was poking his shaggy brown head out the front door. For a young man barely out of his teens, he'd really impressed her with his carpentry skills.

"I need to show you something," he said. "A problem with the rear wall."

Sighing, she nodded. Problems seemed to be in no short supply lately. And naturally he was working on the room that would end up being her living quarters.

She hurried up the steps, taking a final glance down Main Street. Still no Liberty in sight. Beth hoped she hadn't been kept after school for causing trouble. No, she'd show up in a minute. And if not, Beth would stop overreacting and call her. Simple.

"Liberty, it's me again." Beth stopped pacing the small kitchen and looked at the round clock hanging on the wall behind the microwave. "It's six-forty. I'm at home now, so don't go to the boardinghouse. Please call me. I'm very worried."

She dropped her cell on the table. This was the fourth message she'd left, so she wouldn't hold her breath. Except she was so tense that was exactly what she'd been doing. She exhaled slowly, pressing a hand to her chest, not surprised that her lungs actually ached. As soon as she made sure Liberty was all right, Beth was going to strangle her.

The kitchen was too small for her to burn off some adrenaline. The faux-wood microwave stand, its lower shelves crammed with pots and mismatched lids, kept getting in her way. She tried to steer clear of it but failed, ramming her foot against the corner.

"Ouch." She went still, then, balancing on one leg, brought up her foot. "Dammit." The flimsy boot hadn't protected her big toe. She hopped to the chair, sat down and pulled off the boot.

Candace was gone. She'd left a note that she'd picked up an extra shift at the bar in Kalispell where she waited tables part-time. When Beth had called about Liberty, Candace's lack of concern for her missing daughter had pushed every one of Beth's buttons. She was still angry, more so than she'd been in a very long while.

She flexed her toes. They felt better already. But that was it for those boots. Liberty had been sweet to buy them, but they weren't suitable to be worn outside or for work. Beth turned to the clock, then peered out the screen door. It was getting dark. Anger faded to fear. Why wasn't Liberty answering her phone? She'd never ignored Beth's calls before.

It was getting chilly, so Beth got up to close the storm door. She peeked outside first, just as she'd done a dozen times in the past thirty minutes. A black truck with heavily tinted windows slowed in front of the house. She moved down a step and leaned out as far as she could to keep track of where it was headed. The vehicle barely came to a halt when Liberty jumped out of the passenger side and slammed the truck's door. Her face red and furious, she stomped toward the front of the house.

Beth hurried into the yard, realizing she wore only one boot when sharp weeds poked through her sock. That didn't stop her. Before the driver left she wanted to find out what was going on and who'd dropped off her niece. But the truck wasn't going anywhere. Not just yet. The engine was cut, the door opened and in preparation for battle, Beth drew in a deep breath.

When Nathan got out, she nearly choked on the exhale. She could only see the back of his head and broad shoulders, and the truck was different, no ranch logo on the door, but she had no doubt it was him. His expression grim, Nathan slowly turned to face her and shut his door.

"What are— How did—?" Beth glanced back at the house. Liberty was crouched at the window, peeking out from under the curtain. When Beth turned back to Nathan, he was eyeing the neglected lawn and shabby house. "What happened?" she asked, suddenly so tired she wanted to lie down in the middle of the prickly weeds and curl into a ball.

"I didn't expect to see you," he said, looking even bleaker than he had a few seconds earlier. "So Liberty is yours?"

Nodding, she shrugged. "My niece."

"I'm guessing you know about her hobby."

"Yes, I do." The horror of what must've happened finally registered. "Oh, no. She didn't…again?"

Nathan rested his forearms on the side of the truck bed and just looked at her. He didn't answer, but then he needn't bother. The response she dreaded was there in the tightness around his mouth.

"I'm sorry." She swallowed. "I've been calling her since she didn't show up after school." Oh, God, he didn't care about that, she thought, and noticed the light spatter of turquoise paint on his black shirt. *Turquoise?* Really, Liberty? At least it wasn't red from the spray can she'd let the girl keep. Beth felt awful enough. "Was anyone with her? An older boy?"

Nathan shook his head. "Just her."

Beth sighed. "Did you notify the sheriff?"

His gaze ran down the front of her T-shirt and jeans to her toes, then rested on her foot, the one wearing only a stocking. "Is that what you want me to do?" he asked in a quiet voice as he lifted his eyes to her face.

"No." She pushed a hand through her tangled hair. "Yes," she corrected, forcing the word past her lips and briefly closing her eyes. Reporting the violation could mean detention at a Kalispell facility. "Liberty has to understand there are consequences." She glanced back toward the dark house. No lamps had been turned on. If Liberty snuck out the kitchen door...

"I agree," Nathan said. "Though the judge's ruling obviously hasn't done any good."

"True." Beth felt a chill and rubbed her arm. The sun's warmth was gone, leaving behind brisk dusky air. "But it's our job, her mother and I, to get her back on the right path."

"You're cold."

"I'm fine."

"And tense."

"Of course I am. I've been worried sick." Hugging herself, she rocked back on her heels, jerking when something pricked her stockinged foot. "Why wouldn't she answer my calls?"

"I think her phone died." He moved around the truck bed toward her. "Come sit in the cab with me."

"Why?" She stared at his face, and then at the warm steady hand cupping her elbow.

"Because we need to discuss a suitable punishment without you freezing."

It wasn't *that* cold, but she'd rather he think the autumn air had caused her trembling voice. "We could go in the house," she said, dreading the thought of him seeing the inside. As if he wouldn't expect the decor to be thrift-store chic.

He opened the passenger door and helped her up. "It's more private out here." He paused. "I forgot about her mother. Is she home?"

"No." Beth bit off the word before she loaded too much into it. He didn't need to know about her screwed-up sister. "Candace will go along with whatever we decide."

The interior light illuminated Nathan's face. He didn't look angry anymore, not the way he had when she'd first seen him. Though he was obviously still troubled. Probably cataloguing the damage to his property, courtesy of the little hoodlum.

After he'd settled behind the wheel, he blew out a stream of air. The overhead light flickered off, leaving them in a dim murkiness that was eerie yet comforting. Beth cast a glance at the house. It wasn't completely dark. A soft glow came from somewhere in the back, probably Liberty's bedroom.

"She can't see in here. Not with the tinted windows," Nathan said, meeting her eyes when she turned to him.

"I'm more concerned about her slipping out the back door."

"Does she sneak out often?"

"No. Never." Beth rubbed the tension at the base of her neck. "As far as I know anyway. Before I got here she had a lot more freedom. My sister is more permissive. God, Nathan, I can't even begin to tell you how sorry I am."

"It's not your fault."

"Well, yeah, it sort of is…maybe not my fault but my responsibility. When you have a kid, you kind of sign up for this stuff."

"I thought she was your niece."

"She is, but…" Beth laid her head back. "It's hard to

explain." It felt nice sitting in the comfortable leather seat, soothing and warm, though not warm enough. The dashboard and console were clean, the truck even smelled good…a welcome change from drywall dust and a messy house. "Liberty is the reason I moved back. And Candace. They're all the family I have, really."

He let a few seconds tick by in silence, then said, "Let's talk about how we're going to handle this."

She brought her head up, embarrassed she'd revealed anything personal. "Yes, of course," she said, turning to him. "Please don't think I was looking for sympathy or about to unload on you. I wouldn't do that."

"I've got a deal for you," Nathan said, watching her closely. "We come up with a solution that will make Liberty think twice about using a spray can, but won't stress you out."

"I'm not worried about me."

"Tough," he said, reaching across the console. "I am."

6

BETHANY GASPED, HER eyes widening. "What are you—oh. Yes. Right there." Her lids drooping, she dropped her chin as she relaxed under his touch. "Oh, my. If I weren't so broke, I'd hire you as my full-time masseur." She tensed again. "That was a joke."

"Relax." He pressed his fingers into the knot, and ignored her quiet "Ouch."

"The being-broke part," she murmured. "I'm not there yet."

Nathan's intentions had been pure. He'd seen her rubbing the back of her neck. But now, feeling her soft skin and fragile bone structure put him in a different frame of mind.

"It feels better already," she said. "You can stop."

"Is that what you want?"

She hesitated. "No, but we're supposed to be discussing Liberty."

So they were, and better they got that piece of business out of the way. Reluctantly, he broke contact and sat back. "You have anything in mind?"

Bethany looked disappointed, and he almost smiled.

"Well, for starters, she should have to paint whatever wall she defaced. What was it this time?"

"The calving shed. It's isolated from the rest of the buildings and we haven't used it since late spring. If Troy hadn't cut through the north pasture, no one would've seen her." Thinking back, Nathan shook his head. "Doesn't make sense she'd pick the middle of the afternoon when the men are working outside. It was almost as if she wanted to get caught."

"Okay, now, *that* definitely doesn't gel. We had a talk just this morning. I trusted her—" She shook her head in despair. "How about I drop her off at your place every day after school and on weekends until she's repainted the whole shed? Heck, throw in anything else you need painted."

Nathan smiled.

"I'll buy the paint and have her pay me back every last cent." Beth blinked. "Those gallons you had stored with the lumber..."

He didn't say anything. Judging by the sudden slump of her shoulders, she knew the answer.

"I didn't make the connection. I thought it was for a winter project.... It doesn't matter...I'll write you a check for that, too."

"The court's already put it on the restitution list."

"I don't care. You shouldn't have to wait." Bethany stared down at her clasped hands. "Can she start tomorrow?"

He thought about it for a few moments. "Tell you what," he said. "I bet you could use her help at the boardinghouse."

She shook her head, the loose hair from her ponytail fluttering around her face. "I already pay her to do small jobs for me."

"I'm talking about her working for free."

"Half the money I give her goes to victims. Like you. So I don't mind paying her. Look, I understand why you don't want her around the Lucky 7. Or want me there, for that matter, but—"

"Hey."

"I'd wouldn't stay, just drop her off and pick her up, for however long—"

"Stop," he said, and took her hand. Her skin was cold. He waited for her to meet his eyes. Damn, but he wanted to kiss those pretty lips. "I never said I didn't want you at the ranch."

"No, but I knew what you were thinking."

Nathan smiled. "I seriously doubt that."

"Why?"

"You would've slapped me."

She narrowed her eyes, then laughed. When her gaze swept down to their joined hands, he regretted teasing her. She didn't pull away, though maybe she felt obligated, which wasn't what he wanted. "What, then?"

"I don't like seeing you penalized," he said, releasing her hand. "You don't need to be running shuttle service twice a day."

"I'll make sure her mother participates."

Disappointment settled in his gut. On the one hand, he didn't want Beth burdened, on the other, he'd get to see her. "I can drop her off in the evenings when I go to town."

"Come on...you never go to town."

"I was there yesterday."

"Yes, but—" She pressed her lips together and glanced away. "I know you mostly avoid it."

"Not necessarily. I just haven't had a reason to go."

Her gaze shot back to him. She searched his face for a long moment. "But you do now?"

"I might."

"Oh." She smoothed back her hair. "Okay."

Nathan watched her shift nervously, and hoped he hadn't just made a mistake. This afternoon he'd decided to invite her out to dinner, but that was before this thing with her niece. He didn't hold Liberty's actions against Bethany; he just didn't want her to feel pressured.

She gave him a tentative smile. "When do you think you'll know?"

"Depends." He relaxed. "You did promise to buy me a beer."

"Oh. Good. I was worried you'd tell me to take a hike. You looked pretty angry a few minutes ago."

"I was," he admitted. "Your niece has quite a stubborn streak. Hope it doesn't run in the family."

Bethany's lips parted, but for a moment she was speechless. "Um, yeah, well, that doesn't always have to be a bad thing." She gave into a grin. "Some people consider persistence a strength."

"Thanks for the warning."

Her good humor faded. "Did Liberty mouth off to you? Or get nasty?"

He shrugged. "She acted like a typical kid caught in the act...defensive, smug." A couple of times she'd been belligerent, but he didn't have the heart to tell Beth. She looked as if she and her dog had both been kicked. "Woody threatened to put her over his knee. Naturally he'd never touch her but she had him riled."

"Maybe a spanking is exactly what she needs," Bethany muttered. "Okay, I didn't just say that. I really don't believe in hitting a child." She let her head drop back against the headrest, then turned her face to look at him. "Dare I ask what specifically made Woody so mad?"

"She refused to give us her parents' number, made a couple smart-aleck cracks. That's about it. Finally I gave her a choice between going to the sheriff's office or giving me directions here." He paused. "I was shocked to see you walk out."

"Oh, jeez…I about fell over when I saw you. And for a very hairy moment, I wanted to strangle her. Seriously." Bethany sighed. "Her father hasn't been in her life much. And my sister isn't known for dating fine upstanding men. Liberty hasn't had it easy. Basically, though, she's a good kid."

"Thanks to you, I imagine."

"No," she said. "I wish I could say that was true. Until three months ago, I hadn't seen her in quite a while." Her voice had dropped until it was barely a whisper. "Long story."

"Maybe you can tell me about it sometime."

"I don't know about that," she said, her light laugh unable to hide her unease. "It isn't pretty."

"Life seldom sticks to the plan."

"No, it doesn't," she said softly. "I guess you understand that better than most people. I know about you losing your wife, and I'm sorry."

"Thanks." He didn't like talking about Anne. Yes, he missed her and wished things could've been different. She'd died young, and her passing was sad. But for him, the greater tragedy was that so much of her life had been wasted. "So back to Liberty…the offer is still on the table. Use her at the boardinghouse if you want."

"Honestly, I don't have enough for her to do. Not at this stage anyway. Sometimes I pay her to clean the house, which goes against my grain. I think cleaning up after herself should be a given."

He glanced at the small semidark house, wondering if it belonged to Bethany or her sister. Somehow that wasn't where he'd pictured her living. "All right, then, we'll put her to work. I might even throw in mucking stalls."

"Do it." Beth nodded. "Lib had forty hours of community service at Safe Haven. Are you familiar with them?"

"Sure. Good organization. I donate hay every year."

"The two women who run it told me they've seen an improvement in Liberty's attitude, but she hates mucking stalls. It's the chore she dreads the most."

"Everyone does."

"Then, that's exactly what you should have her do. So tomorrow?"

Nathan smiled. "Whatever works best for you."

"She's lucky you're so understanding. Anyone else would've called the sheriff." Beth sighed and tapped her head back against the headrest. "I hope I'm doing the right thing. Maybe circumventing the court is letting her off too easy."

"You care enough to be involved and make tough decisions. That has to matter, especially with only one parent in the picture. Don't be so hard on yourself."

"Oh, I'm not the selfless, loving aunt you might imagine. Another week in that house with those two and I'll be the one the sheriff picks up."

"That bad, huh?"

She let out a heartfelt sigh. "I love them. But living with them, I can do without. The house is small and cluttered and, well…let's just say, as soon as a room is finished at the boardinghouse, I'm moving."

"You won't have much space there either."

"I don't care. It'll be clean and quiet. That's all I need." She shrugged. "At least for now."

Until she eventually decided that moving to Blackfoot Falls had been a bad idea. Nathan wondered how long that would take…two months, a year? Though she wasn't the type to sit back and throw her hands up when things got bumpy. She dug in and searched for solutions. She'd proved that by going after the lumber.

"Oh, and I haven't said anything to Liberty or Candace about me moving yet, so I'd appreciate you keeping that between us."

"I won't say a word."

"Oh, my God, listen to me…you're virtually a stranger and here I'm telling you personal stuff."

"Guess we'll have to do something about that," he said, smiling at her confused look. "Have dinner with me tomorrow. You need the R & R, and we can get to know each other."

"Tomorrow, huh? In Blackfoot Falls?" She seemed surprised, maybe even a little wary.

"I know the timing could've been better…" Damn, he hadn't thought it through. He had every intention of being up front with her, explain that he wasn't looking for a relationship. But did he tell her now or wait until they were having dinner? Hell, all he wanted was an easy friendship and sex. But how did you bring that up to a woman, even someone as worldly as Bethany?

"The timing?" She tilted her head, her expression puzzled. "Oh, you mean because of Liberty. No, I was thinking about how uncomfortable it might be for you to go on a date around here. Everyone would be all eyes and ears watching you get back in circulation for the first time."

"Yeah. No. Not Blackfoot Falls." He had no idea why the word *date* had distracted him. Probably because he'd been with Anne for so long he hadn't *dated* anyone else since high school. In college he'd had sex with other women, but only when he and Anne had called it quits for a while. "Marge's diner is the only place left since the Wagon Wheel closed."

Senior year he'd started going out with Anne. She'd still been young and sweet, and he hadn't pushed for sex. By the middle of the school term she'd assured him she was ready. Sometimes he wondered if losing her virginity to him had been the only thing that bonded them.

"I'm sorry," Beth said, her fretful voice bringing him back. "I made an assumption and now this is awkward."

"What assumption?"

"Dinner being a date, you getting back into that scene for the first time. Take your pick." She hesitated, then found the door handle. "You know what, maybe I'll see you tomorrow when I drop off Liberty."

"Beth, wait." He tried to catch her free hand, missed and gripped her upper arm. "You were right. I was asking you out on a date." He slid his hand to the back of her neck. Her skin was warm and soft, and he could smell the sweet scent of her body. "Cut me some slack, I'm rusty at this sort of thing."

"I'm not so great at it either," she murmured. "Obviously."

He smiled, not buying it for a second. "How are you at kissing?"

GOOD THING HE wasn't waiting for an answer. Startled, at first Beth could only stare. He leaned closer, and she did, too, close enough to feel his breath on her face. He slid his hand from her nape to cup her jaw, his fingers exerting just the right amount of pressure to hold her still and cause something in her stomach to thump.

His lips were soft and firm, moving over hers, in no apparent hurry to do anything more than taste and learn. Her heart began pounding faster when he tested the seam of her lips. She parted them for him and liked that he didn't rush inside her mouth. His gentle exploration gave her time to get used to what was happening, time to enjoy the warm stroke of his tongue against hers.

He moved his hand from her jaw back to a spot behind her neck. Seconds later she felt the release of her ponytail. His fingers slid into her hair, and slanting his head, he kissed her more deeply, more thoroughly.

A warm, heavy feeling was growing in her tummy and spreading to her breasts. Her nipples had already tightened and she placed a hand on his chest, felt the swell of muscle beneath her palm. His mouth left hers to trail light biting kisses down her throat, around to the side of her neck, then continue back to her lips.

Too late she realized she'd been holding her breath. He slipped his tongue back inside, taking possession of her mouth and stealing what little air she had left.

Pushed to her limit, she drew back, gasping and panting. "You sure aren't rusty at kissing," she murmured between gulps of air.

A faint smile curved his mouth. "You okay?"

"I will be."

He stroked his thumb in one slow motion from her cheek down her throat to the neckline of her shirt, his attention riveted to her hair. It had to be a tangled mess, and yet he picked up a few strands to rub between his thumb and forefinger with an odd, almost obsessive fascination.

"Nathan?"

His gaze flickered to her face.

"We have to stop."

"I know," he said, and brushed a kiss at the corner of her mouth.

"I don't want to." Silly of her, but she was disappointed that he hadn't put up a token protest.

His lips moved over hers again, and she completely forgot what she'd been about to say. He didn't try to use his tongue but moved on to her jaw, continuing to press soft kisses to her ear, the warm touch of his damp mouth on her skin making her turn her face into his shoulder to keep from whimpering.

He stopped suddenly. "Damn."

She brought her head up, and turned to follow his gaze out the passenger window toward the house.

Liberty had flipped on the porch light.

Beth groaned and quickly pulled away, the heat from his touch swiftly fading. "How long has it been on?"

"Just now." He caught her wrist and dropped the leather ponytail holder onto her palm. "Sorry I messed up your— Hell, I'm not sorry at all."

Laughing, she ducked away from his marauding hand. "We have to stop."

"I just wanted to touch your hair." He leaned back with a frustrated sigh. "Liberty can't see us…unless she has night-vision goggles."

"Are you familiar with teenagers? Never underestimate them."

Beth remade her ponytail, glancing toward the Rockies. They were still visible, mostly the white snowy peaks, but it had gotten quite dark. "How long have we been sitting out here?"

"Half hour, maybe?"

"Wow, really? She'll probably accuse me of colluding with the enemy."

"What she'd better do is thank you." Nathan's stern

tone brought back the gravity of the reason he was here in the first place. "You're saving her butt from a stiff court sentence. I know Judge Wallace. A kid violating probation and brought before him a third time? He won't hesitate to lock her up to make her think."

The full scope of what Nathan had done finally registered. Obviously he hadn't driven Liberty home as a favor to Beth, because he'd had no idea they were related. But he'd gone out of his way to help a troubled young girl he didn't know, someone who'd victimized him twice. Beth reached over and squeezed his hand. "No, she has *you* to thank for giving her another chance. You could've easily called the sheriff and saved yourself time and gas."

He shrugged, his closed expression telling her he wasn't looking for a pat on the back. "I'll talk with Woody and tell him what we've decided. Once he knows she's your niece he'll cool down and let her work off her punishment."

"Really? Why? He doesn't know me." Beth had just lifted the handle, triggering the overhead light to come on.

Nathan grimaced, glaring at her as if she'd committed a grave injustice. "Why did you do that?"

"Open the door?"

"The light… Now she can see us."

"So…" She saw that he was irritated, but didn't understand why. "We aren't doing anything wrong."

"I was about to." He shook his head and muttered something to himself. "I wanted to kiss you good-night."

"Oh." She bit her lip and pulled the door closed, shutting off the light. "Is it too late?"

"I don't know. She's your niece."

Beth's gaze rested on his tempting mouth, and she

sighed. "I probably have guilt written all over my face as it is. But I'll take a rain check."

His slow smile had her pulse fluttering. "You got it."

"Tomorrow, then. I'll drop her off after school." She opened the door and paused. "Will I see you?"

"I'll be there. We can discuss dinner."

She nodded, perfectly calm on the outside, but inside she was jumpy again. God, but she wanted that kiss. She wanted to crawl over the console and inhale his musky male scent, find out how it would feel to have his arms wrapped around her.

"Beth?" His voice had lowered seductively.

Oh, she *so* couldn't go there again. "How's Liberty's artwork? Any good?"

Nathan snorted. "Do me a favor. Ask Woody."

7

"THIS ISN'T FAIR," Liberty said the moment they turned onto the gravel road leading to the Lucky 7.

"So you've said a dozen times." Or a hundred. Beth had lost count and her patience was wearing thin. They'd had to wait two days for the paint to be delivered. Then, between a major plumbing problem on her end and sick cattle at the Lucky 7, she hadn't seen Nathan. But she'd listened to plenty of Liberty's whining. "Get your feet off the dashboard."

Liberty hesitated, and then with a disgusted sigh, lowered her combat boots to the floor. Folding her arms across her chest, she glared out the window. "I should've been given a choice. Seeing the judge would've been better."

"Really?" Beth stopped the truck in the middle of the road and put it in Park.

From her slumped position, Liberty jerked upright and turned to Beth with wide eyes.

"You want to talk about fair? Do you think I like having to make two round trips out here every day? Or that Mr. Landers wants the disruption of having you there? Frankly, this chance he's giving you is more than you deserve. So knock off the 'I shoulda had a choice' crap. I trusted you, Lib, and you lied to me."

"That can really was for an art project," Liberty muttered. "And if you'd let me go back to court like I wanted, you wouldn't be driving me out here."

Beth held on to her temper, but barely. "I don't know why you're so anxious to face the judge. You're a three-time offender. If you think you'd get off with a slap on the wrist, you're dreaming. Mr. Landers agreeing to this arrangement probably saved you from being thrown in juvie."

Liberty lifted her chin. "Spike told me not to worry—"

"I don't want to hear about Spike. He's wrong." Beth shifted back into Drive but kept her foot on the brake and looked directly into her niece's eyes. "Do you trust me, Lib? Do you believe that I love you and have only your best interests at heart?"

The girl's sulky expression eased, and she nodded.

"Do you think the same is true of Spike?"

Liberty squirmed, hunching her shoulders. "I don't know…" she mumbled. "I haven't known him that long."

"Maybe he does care for you," Beth said gently, not believing it for a second. "But you already know I'm a sure bet. Can't go wrong with me, right?"

Liberty smiled a little. "You're blocking the road."

Beth glanced up ahead, then in the rearview. No one was coming. "Okay, Tootsie Roll, let's hit it."

"You're not supposed to call me that. I'm not a kid anymore."

"Oops, you're right. I'll have to think of a new name."

"Oh, no." Liberty groaned, but her mood had improved. "Can you please just drive? I want to get this over with."

Smiling to herself, Beth released the brake. "I could shorten it to Tootsie."

"What happened to having my best interests at heart?" Liberty muttered, and Beth laughed.

A few minutes later the Lucky 7 came into view. She drove under the wrought iron sign arching over the entrance and parked the truck in the same spot as the first day she'd met Nathan. Knowing she was going to see him sent a little jolt of pleasure zinging through her. She had to really watch herself. Liberty had peppered Beth with questions about what they'd been doing in the truck. Like a good aunt, she'd copped to half the truth.

Beth climbed out and saw Woody with a young cowboy watching several horses mill about between two adjoining corrals. He lifted a hand in greeting and gave her a sign she interpreted to mean he'd be with them shortly. Liberty took her sweet time getting out of the truck, and when Beth saw that she was texting, it required all of her willpower not to pluck the phone from her hand and drop it in the nearest well.

"Turn it off."

The girl looked up, her eyes narrowed in disbelief. "Why?"

"You don't need the distraction."

"I'm not turning off my phone," Liberty said, shaking her head and finishing her text. "I can't."

"You heard your aunt."

Beth recognized Nathan's deep rumbling voice and turned around. He hadn't been there a minute ago.... Her pulse skipped at the sight of him in dark blue jeans and a Western-style tan shirt.

Liberty scowled at him. "I'll put it on silent."

"This isn't a negotiation," Nathan said, his tone calm

but firm. "You either turn off the phone or hand it over to your aunt to be returned when she sees fit."

Liberty snorted. "You can't tell me what to do."

"Lib." Beth tugged at her niece's sleeve. "Don't."

"My ranch, my rules." Nathan stood with his arms crossed, his gaze trained on Liberty and looking much like a man whose authority was never questioned. "What's it going to be?"

Defiance flashed in her face, and then she sighed. "I'll turn it off," she mumbled.

Woody joined them just as Beth said, "And it stays off until I pick you up."

"What?" Liberty's voice rose in indignation, her gaze sweeping from the two men and landing on Beth. "Why can't I use it while I'm waiting for you?"

Woody chuckled. "Don't you worry…we have plenty of work. You won't have time to be standing around waiting." He nodded to Beth. "I'll take over from here."

"Thank you, Woody. I appreciate this so much. We both do," she said, and gave her niece a pointed look. "In fact, Liberty has something she'd like to say to both of you."

She locked gazes with Beth for a moment, her mutinous expression fading to defeat. "I'm sorry for all the trouble I caused," she murmured, staring down at her feet. "Thank you for letting me make it up to you."

Woody started chuckling again, and Beth saw Nathan give him a silent warning.

The older man pretended to clear his throat. "Well, come on, kid," he said, motioning for her to follow him. "I ain't got all day."

"I'm not a kid, and my name is Liberty."

"Fine," Woody muttered, moving at a pace that forced the girl to speed up. "You can call me sir."

"That is so uncool."

"Tough."

As their voices began to fade, Beth turned to Nathan. He was watching her. Not smiling, not even blinking. He just stared, and that flustered her.

"I hope you have a few minutes," she said, her tone all business. "I need to pay you for the paint and supplies."

Amusement flickered in his dark eyes. "Let's go to my office."

"Lead the way," she said, and was confused when he started toward the house. She couldn't say why she assumed he worked out of one of the auxiliary buildings. Or explain her sudden reluctance to follow him. A few days earlier she would've given anything for a peek inside.

Neither of them said a word until they arrived at the small courtyard. Beth noticed a pair of wooden benches that had been hidden from her view the other day. Carefully trimmed grass exposed embedded flagstones that led to the side of the house, and a small tree shaded the sitting area. The rose bushes were now dormant, but she could see the faded remnants of pink blooms.

At the front door, Nathan stopped to scrape his boots on the mat. "Kitty is here today," he said. "She does the cleaning and cooking for me. I leave one speck of dirt on her floor, and she'll find it."

Beth smiled. "Keeps you in line, huh?"

"Hell, she's worse than Woody. Between the two of them, I'm lucky I have any say around here."

"Somehow I doubt that." She took her turn at the mat, but Nathan had opened the door and waved her inside, and she realized mentioning Kitty had been a warning they wouldn't be alone in the house.

"How about something to drink?" he asked, following

her into the foyer. "There's always a pot of coffee brewing and a pitcher of iced tea in the fridge...."

Beth was barely listening. The huge house with its open floor plan held a hint of Spanish influence in its arched doorways and clean white walls. Splashes of color came from the scattered rugs and contemporary artwork. "Wow, this place is amazing." Her gaze bounced from the polished wood floor to the interesting mix of contemporary and antique furniture.

A beautiful cherry console table sat in the middle of the foyer. She lightly trailed her fingertips over the gleaming wood, imagining a large vase of fresh-cut flowers sitting dead center. She spotted a mark left by her fingers and yanked her shirt hem from her jeans to wipe the smudge.

"What are you doing?"

"I just had to touch. Jeez, I know better. Sorry."

Nathan stopped her furious rubbing by taking her hand and drawing her away from the table. "It's okay," he said. "This isn't a museum. You can touch."

Her gaze met his, then lowered to his mouth, slid to his clean-shaven chin and finally settled on his chest. Oh, she wanted to touch, all right. "Anywhere?"

He let go of her, freeing his hand to slowly run up her arm. Something mysterious and promising gleamed in his eyes. Something that made her belly clench. "Anywhere," he said, his voice rough and sexy.

Beth inhaled deeply, unsure how to respond. She knew what she'd like to do, just not what was acceptable.

"I thought I heard you come in."

Beth yanked away and whirled around to see a short, slender woman hurrying from the back of the house. Her stocking feet padded silently on the wood floor, but luckily she wasn't close enough to have heard or witnessed their brief tête-à-tête. She smoothed her pixie-cut salt-and-pepper hair and smiled.

"I'm Kitty," she said. "You must be Beth."

Nathan snorted a laugh. "How do you know who she is? You and Woody must be on speaking terms again."

"Oh, hush." Kitty waved dismissively, then paused, a glimmer of mischief entering her blue eyes. "I'd sooner converse with a mule. And you can tell him I said that," she added with a decisive nod. When she turned to Beth, the smile was back on her face. "It's so nice to have another woman around the place."

Beth immediately tensed. "I'm only here on business," she said, automatically glancing at Nathan, who seemed no more concerned than if they'd been discussing the weather.

Kitty bent over to pick up a small dead leaf someone had tracked inside. "Why don't you two come with me to the kitchen for something cool to drink?"

"Not today," Nathan said. "Beth and I have something we need to discuss. Maybe another time."

"Will you be in your office?" Kitty asked with a trace of eagerness. "I can bring in some coffee or tea."

"Beth?" Nathan touched her arm, the action drawing Kitty's interest. "Would you like something?"

"No, thanks. I'd rather we settle up so I can get back to town." She unconsciously patted her back jeans pocket, but her checkbook wasn't there. Alarmed, she tried the other pocket. "I could've sworn—I must've left it in the truck."

Kitty stared blankly at her.

Nathan's gaze lingered on her backside, then swept up to her face. With a faint smile, he gestured to a short hall off the foyer. "My office is this way."

She opened her mouth to explain she had to go look

for her checkbook, but something in his darkened eyes made her doubt her ability to speak. This wasn't good. It seemed Kitty already might have the wrong idea about them. They needed privacy to get whatever they had to off their chests.

His office was huge, almost the size of Candace's rented house. A massive desk, dark wood, maybe mahogany, sat toward the back of the room and shelves of books made up two walls. All the furniture was very masculine, from the pair of brown leather club chairs to the oversize tweed sofa. He even had a stone fireplace. The French doors, though, that was surprising.

"Wow, you could live in here." The polished wood floor made Beth pause, wondering if she should take off her boots. She'd hate to leave scuff marks.

Nathan came up behind her. "What's wrong?"

"I don't want to mess up your floor."

"You're fine," he said, touching the small of her back. Probably trying to get her to keep moving. But her legs stopped working, and she froze, certain he could hear her heart pound wildly at the feel of his warm breath on her neck. "Beth?"

"Woody seemed in good spirits. I assume he's okay with our arrangement. Regarding Liberty…you know, for her to do the painting herself. I'm sure that means more work for him since he'll want to keep tabs on her. Oh, I meant to ask, did you receive your lumber delivery?"

Her sudden rambling was met with silence. Then she felt his hands on her shoulders, and he gently turned her to face him. It took her several long moments before she forced herself to meet his dark unreadable eyes.

"Woody knows you're invested in straightening her out, so he's okay with the decision. I think he'll end up being good for her since he won't take any guff." Nathan frowned. "Now, you mind telling me why you're so nervous?"

"My checkbook," she said, swallowing. "I really thought I had it on me. Could be in the truck but I might've lost it."

"Is that the only thing bothering you?" He waited for her jerky nod, then removed his hands from her shoulders. "Look, if you've changed your mind about having dinner with me, I'm a big boy. I can take it."

"Are you kidding?" She felt the heat rise in her face. Okay, so maybe she could've toned down her reaction.

"Good." A slow smile curved his mouth. "I lied. I would've wailed like a baby. How about tonight?"

God, she loved the man's confidence. "Sounds perfect."

He slid his hand around to the small of her back and drew her closer. "You have anyplace in mind?"

"Depends," she said, tilting her head back to look at him. "Are we really going to eat?"

Nathan looked momentarily startled, then his eyes darkened with pure male satisfaction. Tightening his arm around her, he pulled her against him. He was already getting hard, the rigid proof of how much he wanted her making her dizzy.

She slid her hands up his chest to his shoulders, then down to clutch his flexing biceps. For two restless nights she'd relived the feel of his hard muscles under her palms. Dreamed about how amazing he would look naked.

He brushed his lips over hers. It was a sweet kiss, not at all the one she'd expected, and then he caught her lower lip between his teeth. After the first gentle nibble, his tongue swept inside her mouth, circling and teasing, until she started to squirm from the excitement rippling through her.

The hand on her back lowered to the curve of her bottom. His other arm came around and he cupped her backside with both hands, lightly squeezing, molding her against him. His low growl made her shift and move her head in search of an angle that would allow them to breathe. Instead, he deepened the kiss.

She had no complaint. Not while she was wrapped in his strong arms, feeling weightless and a little woozy, without a care in the world.

Except she had plenty to worry about. Her niece, for instance, the main reason Beth had moved to Blackfoot Falls. And, oh, God, Liberty was just outside.... Beth stiffened and Nathan immediately slackened his hold.

He lifted his head, his lips damp and parted as he stared down at her. Neither of them spoke right away. Her heart was still pounding, and his seemed to be keeping pace. She relaxed her grip on the back of his neck and let her palms slide to his shoulders.

"Liberty," she said finally. "She asked why we took so long the other night in your truck. I told her we had trouble coming to terms. She can't know about this...."

"This?" As his gaze lowered from her face, his frown faded to pure lust.

She glanced down. He was staring at the stiff peaks straining against her blouse. Reverently he touched each breast, then brushed his thumbs over her hard nipples. She gasped, the contact achingly acute, even through the two layers of fabric.

His eyes briefly closed before he looked up. He didn't bother hiding the slight tremor in his hands when he cradled her face. "I'm listening," he murmured. "I am. I'm trying."

"I know." She had to smile. He sounded so sweet and

earnest. "I want this, too. I want you—" she whispered, cut short by a kiss that defied sweet or earnest.

His mouth claimed hers, his tongue thrusting inside, hungry, impatient, demanding a response she eagerly gave. Yanking two snaps free, she slipped her hand inside his shirt before she realized what she was doing.

She dragged her mouth away from his, but he followed her retreat, trying to capture her lips again, forcing her backward until she gave him a light shove.

"Nathan, stop." She let out a small laugh, and he frowned. "One more slipup and we each take a corner."

The sound he made was more grunt than agreement, though at least he pulled back. And gave her a great view of the exposed wedge of muscled chest. She sighed, feeling as frustrated as he looked.

"You'll have to..." She motioned with an unsteady hand. "You know...button up."

He glanced down, unconcerned. "Why?"

"So I can concentrate," she practically snapped at him, which seemed to improve his mood.

While he fastened his shirt, he moved to his desk and sat on the edge, then crossed his arms. He was still hard—of course he was. And, what, he didn't think *that* would be a distraction?

"Let's face it...I doubt either of us is looking for anything more than good conversation and sex," she said, pleased to see his dark brows lift in surprise. "So there's really no reason for anyone to know our business. Agreed?"

He hesitated, then nodded.

They'd already touched on this subject, so to speak, and she hadn't intended to remind him quite like this, but then she hadn't expected them to get carried away. "Any thoughts on how to stay under the radar?"

"Just past the junction to Kalispell there's an old line shack. You can leave your truck parked behind it and I'll pick you up. Does 7:00 work for you?"

"Um…sure." If he'd intended to shock her with his well thought-out plan, he'd succeeded. Though he didn't look particularly smug.

Just sexy.

And hot.

His eyes glittered with promise. And his erection? Still front and center.

8

THE REST OF the afternoon sped by in a mad rush. Liberty had called to be picked up at 5:45 p.m., a duty Beth had delegated to Candace, who'd predictably complained. Not that Beth gave a damn. She'd needed time for some personal grooming she'd let slide. So she'd mentioned she was going to Kalispell and that was it.

Before they got back, Beth slipped on a short denim skirt, a stretchy top and a crazy-cute pair of red Jimmy Choo shoes with a ridiculously high heel, and was out the door.

At 6:55 p.m. she parked her truck behind the old shack, just as Nathan had instructed. She'd barely had time to check her hair and makeup when a pair of headlights swept the dark, scrubby landscape behind her.

She recognized Nathan's truck, and within seconds he was right there, opening her door and offering her a hand. His hair was damp and combed back, his jaw clean shaven. Her silly heart did that little fluttering thing even before their palms met.

"You look great," he said, running his gaze down her scoop-neck shirt, lingering a moment on the short hem of her denim skirt and then again on her shoes and matching red toenails.

Oddly, he didn't seem pleased.

"But?"

He looked up. "Nothing," he said, shrugging. "You look incredible. I'm not sure you'll like where I'm taking you."

"We're not staying here, are we?" She glanced at the rundown shack and smiled.

Nathan bit off a laugh. "Let's go."

Beth let him help her to the truck even though she didn't need it. The ground was uneven but not too soft, and she was good in heels. He brushed a soft kiss at the corner of her mouth before closing the passenger door. So stupid to have worn lip gloss. She might've gotten a better kiss. Though the night was still young.

As soon as they were on the road, she looked back to make sure her small pickup couldn't be seen from the highway.

"That shack was put there before the highway came through," Nathan said. "Nothing to worry about." He leaned over and turned off the radio, although the light from the center console stayed on.

Country music had been playing in the background, low enough it had barely registered. But then, she was too busy eyeing the flexing of his thigh muscles when he engaged the clutch.

"Leave it on if you want. I don't mind," she said, finally noticing that his jeans were black and his white shirt was a traditional button-down and not Western. "Where are we going?"

"My place." Briefly taking his eyes off the road, he glanced at her. "I think it's our best bet for now."

"The Lucky 7? Seriously?"

"Are you disappointed?"

She was staring with her mouth open. "No, it's not that—I thought we agreed to keep things on the down low."

"My men got paid today. Most of them are at the Watering Hole or in Kalispell. Woody's playing poker with a couple of the old-timers in the bunkhouse. Nobody will know you're there."

"Someone is bound to see me."

"The garage is attached to the house."

She had to think about this. She really did need this thing between them to be private. Candace, with her unhealthy attachments to the wrong men, was a bad enough example. Liberty didn't need to see Beth having a fling, especially with someone who was cutting Liberty a break—she didn't want her niece to think she was buying favors.

"All right, I see you're hesitant about my place," Nathan said. "So let's talk about it. Kalispell is still an option. It's a lot bigger than Blackfoot Falls. That doesn't eliminate the risk of being seen, but it's more likely we wouldn't."

"No, I trust you know best about this. I'm probably being overly cautious. Only because of Liberty. She's never really had a good role model." Beth wasn't in the habit of walking into a prearranged sexual relationship. What if tonight went badly? What if his kinks and hers didn't mesh? This thing between them could be over in an hour, never to be repeated.

To her relief, he let the subject drop and they made small talk for the remainder of the ride. Before she knew it, they were on the grounds of the Lucky 7, then pulling into the garage and parking next to a green Range Rover.

Still, she didn't breathe easy until they'd entered the

house through the laundry room and ended up in the big modern kitchen. It was as gorgeous as the other parts of the house, with gleaming stainless-steel appliances and tons of beautiful peachy-brown granite. Someone sure liked to cook. As if the crazy expanse of countertops weren't enough, there was also an oversize island, an additional sink and a grill with warming tray.

A lot of thought had been put into the design, not just in the kitchen but throughout what she could see of the rest of the house. One casually elegant room spilled into the next. From the kitchen she saw a massive stone fireplace, two large sofas and a flat-screen TV that was so big it had to be brand-new technology.

"I hope you're hungry," Nathan said, tossing his keys on the counter near the phone. "Kitty made enough food for the whole county."

"Did she know you were having company?"

"Not that I'm aware of." He ran a hand through his hair and frowned. "She might suspect, but you don't have to worry about her gossiping."

"I'm glad. It seems I'm under the careful watch of everyone in Blackfoot Falls. Makes sense, since I'm the new kid in town." Beth moved closer to the stove and sniffed the large covered casserole that sat on top. "Please tell me this is lasagna."

Looking up just in time to see his rugged jaw clench, food slipped her mind for a second. Damn, he had a great face. Great body. Great everything. "Go ahead and have a look," he said.

She did just that, peeling back the foil at the corner. Wow. "I haven't eaten all day. I'm starving."

"You wear heels that high often?"

She glanced at him, startled. "Not lately. I wouldn't have worn them tonight except—" Her thoughts scattered when he started toward her. She leaned back and braced her hands on the counter.

Something dark and predatory flared hot in his eyes. His gaze briefly swept her shirt, the stretchy material pulled tight across her breasts. Whatever he had in mind, there wasn't a lasagna in the whole world that could compete. Swallowing, she waited for him to make his next move.

He stopped short of touching her. "Except what?"

Blinking away the brain fog took a moment. "I usually can't wear them on dates," she said, her voice low, barely audible. "They make me too tall for most men."

"You are tall," he whispered, putting his hands on her waist and meeting her eyes. Then he lowered his gaze to her mouth. "How about some wine? Or something harder, if you prefer."

"Wine is good."

"White or red?"

"Don't care."

"Music?" His grip on her waist tightened for an instant and then relaxed. "I have country, jazz, classic rock…" He cleared his throat as he stepped back. "You could go choose something while I open a bottle of merlot." He yanked open the closest drawer and rummaged around. "The CDs are in the den," he said, motioning with his chin toward the room with the TV.

"Okay." She could've sworn he'd been about to kiss her. Was it the stupid gloss holding him back? She'd forgotten about it and took a quick swipe with her tongue. It felt as if she'd already licked most of it off.

He let out a laugh, or maybe it was a groan. "You're not making this easy."

"What? What did I do?" she asked, catching his arm when he turned away.

"I'm trying to be a gentleman."

Beth didn't understand. "That's—that's very nice." She let go. "I think."

Slowly he brought out a pair of wineglasses from an upper cabinet. "Not interested in music?" he asked without looking at her.

"Oh, music. Right." Still confused, she started toward the den. He obviously had no trouble initiating a kiss. He'd proved that in his office earlier.

She spotted the rows of CDs right away, neatly stored in racks built into the wall and grouped by genre and artist. It was quite a collection. Along with a selection of DVDs…a whole bunch of them. A lot were old films, some black-and-white, but the musical classics were a surprise. She wouldn't have guessed they were Nathan's. They must have belonged to his wife.

Beth turned around and studied the room. The Roman shades, designer furniture, art pieces…even the lamps had a different feel from the way Nathan's office was decorated. All this was his wife's work. Beth would bet anything that nothing had been changed or moved in three years.

Now she understood why she'd had trouble reading Nathan earlier. Having her here in his wife's domain probably felt awkward for him.

"Finding anything you like?" he called from the kitchen.

She spun back to the CD selection. "Bob Seger, if that's okay with you."

"Sounds good."

It was the first name Beth saw. She started the CD, and relaxed at the deep, raspy voice. Too late, she realized she could've loaded more than one CD, then was distracted by the floor-to-ceiling shelves to the left of the fireplace where a framed photo caught her attention.

The beautiful woman with the blue eyes and upswept auburn hair had to be his wife. Beth ducked to get a closer look without handling the intricate silver frame. Boy, did the camera love her. With her flawless skin and perfect bow lips, she could've been a model.

Beth switched her gaze to the next photo. It was the same woman, only this photo was candid, a full body shot, and she was really petite. Probably no more than five feet. So much for a modeling career. She was still beautiful, and clearly the type of woman Nathan preferred. It shouldn't have mattered to Beth. And it didn't. As long as the sex was good, that was all she cared about....

"Here's your wine."

At the sound of his voice directly behind her, she nearly jumped into the next decade.

"I called from the kitchen. I guess you didn't hear me over the music. You okay?"

She gave a jerky nod, realized her hand had flown to her throat and lowered it to take the glass from him. "Thanks. I was just checking out your books." Beth sighed. "And the photos."

Nathan smiled. "Yes," he said, not looking the least upset.

"Yes?" she echoed, not knowing what he meant.

"Those two photos are of Anne. My late wife. I'm sure you're curious, and I wanted you to know it's all right to ask."

Beth glanced back at the other framed photographs scattered along three shelves. She hadn't paid attention to them, but something he'd said made her look more closely. The rest of the pictures had to be of Nathan's family—the resemblances were too strong not to be. There were no more shots of Anne, just the two. And not a single one of Nathan and Anne together.

"Are those your brothers?" Beth asked, hoping he wouldn't think she'd fixated on his dead wife.

He picked up a photo of two teenagers wearing football jerseys and big grins. They were holding up a trophy, or more aptly, playing a game of tug-of-war with it. Nathan grinned. "How could you tell?"

Smiling back, she relaxed. "When was it taken?"

"They were still in high school." He studied the photograph, the fondness in his eyes tinged with sadness. Then he blinked and it was gone. "About thirteen years ago."

"So they're both younger than you."

"Clint is two years behind me," he said, returning the photo to the shelf. "Seth is the baby."

"I'm sure he loves you referring to him exactly like that."

"Hell, he had a few names for me I wasn't too fond of."

"Care to share?"

A faint smile curving his mouth, he took her glass from her.

"Hey…I've only had two sips."

He set their glasses next to the CD player and turned the volume down a bit.

She knew what he was going to do and beat him to it by sliding her arms around his neck. "I thought we were going to eat."

"This is the appetizer." His hands went to her waist and he pulled her against him as he bent his head.

His lips were warm and sure as they moved over her mouth. She pushed her fingers into his hair and felt his tongue run across the seam of her lips. He kept going, tracing the curve of her jaw with the tip of his tongue, then finding that sensitive spot where her neck and shoulder met.

He brushed her hair out of the way, letting it fall down her back, then followed the scoop of her neckline with his mouth. Pleasure shimmered through her. The musky scent of his heated skin was like a drug invading her system, making her weak and lethargic. She wound her arms tighter around his neck, hanging on to him for support, clutching at his hair. She hadn't intended to force his head up.

Nathan pulled his mouth away and looked at her. His lips were damp, his eyes dark with desire.

Beth was starting to lean in for more when her stomach gurgled loudly enough they both heard it.

He closed his eyes for a second before letting her go. "We don't have to do anything tonight but eat and talk. I'd meant to say that before."

"I'm worried you're finding it more difficult having me here than you thought." She carefully studied his face, but he wasn't giving anything away. "If that's the case, I've heard I make a decent friend."

"You always run around saving people?"

Now she saw that he didn't seem upset at all. Maybe he was trying to be a gentleman and not rush her, just as he'd said.

"As a matter of fact, yes. Except I used to get paid for it."

"What is it you used to do?"

"Event planner. I started out arranging corporate meetings, but we did some weddings and parties as a favor to corporate clients. The money was ridiculously good, so we branched out."

"We?" He brought down plates from an upper cabinet. "You had a partner?"

"No, Fritz was my boss. He taught me everything I know about the business. I gave him plenty of notice before leaving, but he acts as if I deserted him." She leaned a hip on the island and sipped her wine. "He's also convinced I'll come to my senses and ask for my job back."

"Think you will?"

She laughed. "I might wise up and lock Liberty in her room until she's thirty, but go back to event planning? Not a chance. After living out of a suitcase for ten years, I've had enough." She noticed the three bar stools pushed under the lip of the island. "Should I set the table, or do you want to eat here?"

He seemed distracted, then glanced toward the open dining room where a beautiful cherry table with eight upholstered chairs had center stage. A matching china hutch had been placed against the wall shared with the kitchen.

Beth pressed her lips together. "Did you forget you have a dining room table?"

"Go ahead…laugh."

She blinked. "You did? Seriously?" She searched his face. He had to be teasing her.

"I usually eat in my office," he muttered, making a racket pulling out the silverware and keeping his back to her.

"Nathan."

"Mind getting the napkins? They're in the drawer to your right."

Watching him do his best to ignore her, she struggled between dropping the subject and needling him.

She walked around the island, recalling how he'd had trouble finding the corkscrew. A weird feeling settled in the pit of her stomach. Had he become a stranger in his own home? As soon as she saw his expression she knew. "You weren't kidding, were you?"

"Why is this an issue?" he muttered.

"I'm sorry. It's not. Your house is so amazing, and all these huge windows… It's dark so I can't see the view, but I bet it's spectacular. It feels as if I'm at a fancy retreat or a spa. I could never take a house like this for granted—" She stopped. Winced at the implication.

Nathan just shook his head and picked up the lasagna. He didn't seem angry or annoyed or much of anything. For a second she thought she saw a hint of amusement in his face, but she wasn't sure.

"You know what, Bethany?" he said, stopping right in front of the table. "You're a fascinating woman. I'm glad you're here. But I have to confess, sometimes I just don't know what the hell to do with you."

His confession did wonderful things for her nerves. She hadn't felt so flustered on a date since her early teens. Maybe it was because she'd expected a discreet dinner and a more discreet motel? Or maybe it was the fact that he was so damned enigmatic.

On the other hand, she'd always liked puzzles.

9

NATHAN CARRIED THE food to the table, silently acknowledging that it had been too long since he'd been with a woman who wasn't Anne.

Like any married couple, they'd fallen into a routine. He and Anne had disagreed, but only over petty things. Her eyes would fill with tears and he'd let her have her way. When it came to ranch business or finances, she'd just smile and tell him to do whatever he thought best, so he'd quit trying to involve her.

He watched Beth pop a cherry tomato into her mouth, then pick up their salad plates and close the knife drawer with her hip. He doubted she'd have trouble expressing an opinion. Hell, he expected she had a whole lot of them. And if they disagreed over something, she wouldn't hesitate to go toe-to-toe with him. He kind of liked the idea, though he didn't have much experience dealing with a strong-willed woman.

She leaned in front of him to set his salad on the placemat and he got a tantalizing whiff of her vanilla-scented hair. "Oh, I forgot the salad dressing," she said, brushing against his thigh and chest when she straightened.

The accidental touch brought a soft bloom of color to

her cheeks. Now that was unexpected. The sudden tightening in his groin was not.

"I'll get it," he said, and pulled out her chair. "You sit."

She hesitated, then started to squeeze past him.

He kissed her upturned face. Just a light peck on her cheek, another on the tip of her nose. He used a little more pressure on her parted lips.

When Beth finally needed to take a breath, she let out a soft gasp, her sweet warm breath teasing his chin and nostrils. "We aren't going to eat, are we?"

"We are." He forced himself to back up. Dammit, he'd promised himself he wouldn't rush the evening.

"I really don't care—"

"I do." He didn't wait for her to sit but headed back to the kitchen. "Anything else we need while I'm here? Steak sauce?"

"Um, no, we're having the lasagna."

"Right." He heard her soft laugh and just shook his head. Here he was, a grown man, thirty-four years old, and he was gonna disgrace himself tonight. He just knew he would. He'd be lucky if he didn't shoot his wad before he got her bra off. And wouldn't that be a hell of a thing.

"Thank you." Beth took the bottle of dressing he brought to the table. "You know we could've eaten in the kitchen, right? I was only teasing you."

"Come on, you wore high heels and everything. Don't tell me you weren't expecting to eat at a table."

"What you didn't know was that while you were in the kitchen, I took my shoes off." Her laugh was low, throaty and sexy as hell. "But eating dinner without plates…that's where I draw the line."

"Here I thought you were the adventurous type," he said, and she gave him a sassy smile that had him serving up the lasagna real quick.

She dug in, not wasting time cutting dainty pieces or trying to scrape off any of the rich melted cheese. Instead, she twirled her fork to make sure she didn't lose a single stringy morsel.

Taking his first bite made him realize he was famished. Used to eating alone, he had to remind himself not to start shoveling in his food. After three sizable forkfuls, he paused for a sip of wine.

Beth was awfully quiet, staring out into the darkness while she ate. He hoped he hadn't dampened her mood. Though he had a feeling he'd made several wrong turns tonight.

"I don't take this house for granted," he said, and when she put down her fork, he realized he should've waited to set the record straight. "I love this place, I always have. The Lucky 7 started with seven acres of scrub brush. I built it from the ground up, and the house was every bit as important to me as the rest of the ranch."

"I'm so sorry, Nathan. I shouldn't have said what I did."

"That didn't bother me. That's not why I brought it up." He wiped his mouth with his napkin. "Since I was thirteen I knew I wanted my own ranch. I left college a year early so I could get on with building something for myself. My grandfather left me and my brothers each seven acres. He probably figured we'd all end up staying on the Whispering Pines and working with my dad, but I appreciated the chance to see what I could do on my own.

"On breaks from school I used to come out here and mark the ground where I wanted the barn, stables, corrals…everything. Turned out some of the buildings weren't in practical locations, so I had to tinker with the plans. But not the house. That never changed. I knew exactly where I wanted it and purposely built it at this angle. On the east side every room has a view of the sun coming up. On the other side you can watch it set behind the Rockies."

"Quite an undertaking for someone so young."

"I knew what I wanted and stayed focused." He took another bite of his food, hoping she'd do the same. She sipped her wine but didn't touch her fork.

"You must've married young," she said, then looked as if she wished she hadn't, which could mean his suspicion was accurate. She thought he was having trouble letting go of Anne.

He shrugged, continued to chew. "Anne was two years behind me. We waited a year after she graduated from college, mostly so I could get the Lucky 7 off the ground. I was twenty-four when we tied the knot. In retrospect… yeah, that was too young." Nathan could see questions forming in her eyes. "Your food's getting cold."

"This stuff is so good I'd eat it half-frozen," she said, and narrowed her gaze. "It's scary but I'm kinda serious."

He grinned. "I'll be sure to pass that on to Kitty."

"Um, what part of keeping this thing secret don't you get?"

"Ah, my bad."

"Look, you know I'm worried about how Lib would react, but I'm keeping this quiet for you, too."

"I appreciate that, and while I don't plan on broadcasting anything, I'm not concerned with Kitty or Woody finding out. Believe me, they know how I feel about small-town gossips. They're trustworthy and won't stick their noses in too far."

Beth nodded, her gaze fixed on the fingertip she was running along the rim of her wineglass. "Nice crystal," she said absently, then blinked and glanced around. "Everything is very…nice. You have wonderful taste."

"I didn't have anything to do with the decorating. And for the record, I hadn't forgotten I have a table.... I use the kitchen every day to make coffee. Everything in the house, with the exception of my office, was Anne's taste."

He left out that Anne had bought him pottery and brass doodads for his office. They were gone now. He'd told Kitty to take whatever she wanted, and she hadn't argued, not after he'd hurled a ceramic bowl against the wall in a fit of rage. Scared the bejesus out of the poor woman. She'd had no way of knowing he'd found Anne's birth control pills a few minutes earlier. For two years his *loving* wife had led him to believe they were trying to start a family. Just another lie in a string of many.

Beth touched his hand. "Nathan? You okay?"

"Not used to talking so much at one time." He drained his glass. "How about we finish eating, and then I'll show you the rest of the house?"

"Perfect," she murmured, and picked up her fork.

For the next five minutes they spoke very little and ate quickly. Nathan finished off his meal. He hoped the food would give him stamina, both before and after he got her naked.

By the time they cleared the table, every move they made was laced with the spark that had started this whole thing. Finally, he couldn't stand it another second.

He pulled her against him as he bent his head. She automatically lifted her lips. He brushed them with what started as a light kiss, but quickly became more. She tasted like wine and temptation, and it was hard to resist lifting her onto the table and having her right there. Instead, he eased back, leaned down and kissed her breast through her clingy top and bra.

"Very sneaky," she said, shuddering in his arms. "Let's see what else you have up your sleeve."

That was all the coaxing he needed. He hurried them both toward his bedroom, but halfway down the hall he pulled down the zipper of her denim skirt. Gasping, she retaliated by jerking his shirt from his jeans. She yanked again and two buttons popped off and hit the wall.

"Oops." Her eyes widened. She covered her mouth. "I forgot they weren't snaps."

He drew her hand away and took advantage of her parted lips, slipping his tongue inside, mating it with hers and savoring her sweetness. Her body molded to him and her sexy moans went straight to his cock.

He was already hard. Too hard. Jesus. He'd known this would happen. He had to cool it, get hold of himself. Not behave like a stupid, impatient kid. But she was soft and warm and eager, her mouth continuing to seek his when he tried to draw back.

So much for good intentions. He freed the hem of her shirt and slid his hand underneath. The smooth feel of her taut, silky skin nearly did him in. He cupped the weight of her breast, frustrated with the bra preventing him from fingering her nipple. This was crazy. They could've been naked by now.

Lifting his head, he broke the kiss and moved his hands to her shoulders. She stared up at him in dazed confusion, then blinked. Her lips were pink and a little swollen. Temper sparked in her eyes and she went for another button.

"Wait," he said, his hoarse laugh meeting a glare. "We're almost—"

"I can do two things at once," she said, making a grab for his shirt. But he caught her wrist and pulled her the rest of the way to his bedroom. He flipped on the light switch and the nightstand lamps filled the room with a dim glow. The bed was already turned down, the beige-

and-brown comforter draped over a wing chair. Something made her giggle.

"What?" Watching her, he finished unbuttoning his shirt and shrugged out of it. Her attention was drawn to his chest, then down his belly. "I have a favor to ask," he said, his voice a low, rough rumble.

"What's that?" she asked, her gaze lifting from the front of his jeans to his eyes.

"Take off your top for me?"

She smiled and slowly pulled up the hem, exposing a satiny peach-colored bra. Then she drew the shirt over her head. Her honey-blond hair fell in waves around her slim shoulders.

"Beautiful," he whispered, then looked her in the eyes again. "Dammit."

"What's wrong?"

"Boots. Don't go anywhere." He sat at the foot of the bed to take the damn things off. He couldn't stop watching Beth, though, as she looked around the room. Her gaze paused on the antique armoire and matching dresser. He'd never taken off boots so fast in his life. Once they were tossed aside, he captured her hand, tugged her close enough to stand between his spread legs.

Every instinct wanted him to finish stripping her, lay her down on her back and cover her body with his. It wasn't easy, but he paused to savor the beauty of her pale skin, the slight quiver of her lower lip, enjoy the satisfaction of her body starting to arch toward him.

He drew her bra strap down her arm and kissed her shoulder. The satiny smooth feel of her made the need to have her beneath him more urgent. He unclasped her bra, then sucked in a breath when the fabric fell away from her breasts. Her flushed nipples had tightened into rosy buds. He pulled her skirt down her hips, ready to explode when she helped by doing a slight shimmy that made her breasts jiggle.

Quickly he finished stripping off her skirt until she stood before him in only her skimpy peach-colored panties. She inhaled deeply, and her bare breasts thrust at him. He touched them, brushing his thumbs across her aroused flesh. Then, when he couldn't stand it a moment longer, he put his arms around her and drew a nipple into his mouth.

BETH COULDN'T SEEM to stop trembling. Nathan's arms tightened, steadying her. She caught her breath as he suckled harder. Realizing she was digging her nails into his shoulders, she curled her fingers into her palms.

Lifting his mouth from her breast, he stared at her with glazed eyes before his gaze moved to the fisted hands hanging at her sides. After returning them to his shoulders, he rubbed his palms down her back until he cupped her bottom. He rolled his tongue over her other nipple and she shuddered, whimpered, nearly begged. His skin was hot. So was his hungry mouth, and her hips automatically rocked against him.

With a husky groan, he lifted her into his arms and she clung to him as he carried her around to the side of the bed and laid her on the bronze-colored sheets. He touched her face, let his fingers trail between her breasts, over her rib cage, down to her belly, his gaze running half a heartbeat behind.

Normally she preferred smooth chests. His was the exception. Soft black hair peppered the olive skin between his small brown nipples and ran down in a narrow line to his flat, ridged belly. He had the perfect amount of muscle definition, and she was having trouble dragging her eyes away. But she had to see the rest of him, and surged up to tug at his open jeans.

"Hold on," he said. "We'll get there." He cupped her shoulders, his hands firm but gentle, urging her back to the sheets. He smiled and kissed her mouth, using his tongue to gain entrance. Her eyes drifted closed, but she opened them when he broke the kiss and muttered a curse.

Beth found him leaving the bed, tugging down his jeans. "Want help?"

"No. Stay right there."

Expecting a show, she was disappointed he hadn't taken his boxers off at the same time. But then he was bending over her, and she felt the warm pressure of his lips on the side of her neck, the rough pad of his thumb circling her nipple, the dampness growing between her thighs.

Before she knew it he'd quickly, efficiently stripped her panties down her legs. She let out a gasp that he caught in his mouth. He swirled his tongue around hers as he slid his hand back up, slowly skimming the outside of her calves, making her breath catch when he moved to the inside of her thigh. Instinctively she squeezed her legs together. He deepened the kiss, keeping his hand completely still until she relaxed.

The first brush of his fingers against her damp flesh made her buck wildly. He joined her on the bed, dropped a quick kiss on her thigh and positioned himself between her legs. She started to protest the presence of his boxers when he bent his head and stroked his tongue against her. Her startled gasp was nothing compared to how high she arched off the bed. So high he gripped her hips to keep from breaking contact. His mouth was hot, his tongue sure, and he seemed determined to taste every inch of her.

She bucked and squirmed against the fiery sensation burning inside her, rushing like lava through her veins and filling her chest and limbs. She hadn't expected this, hadn't even liked it very much in the past, but with Nathan…she was shockingly close to climaxing.

His tongue circled, dipped and flicked, fast then slow, fast again. It drove her crazy, bringing her to the brink over and over, teasing her, confusing her. She wanted the sensations to go on forever; she wanted to explode with release. When he lifted one leg over his shoulder and changed the angle, the next swipe of his tongue sent the first bolt of shimmering heat through her body.

She couldn't breathe. Couldn't move. And then she couldn't stop moving. No matter how hard she bucked with the relentless spasms, his mouth stayed with her. He knew exactly how much pressure to use, when to firm the tip of his tongue as if they'd been doing this same dance forever. When she was certain she couldn't take anymore, she clawed at his hair, searched for her voice so she could tell him to stop, then fell back in complete wonder when the next wave swept her toward even greater pleasure.

Finally she went limp, her unsteady breath coming in labored pants. "Nathan?" She touched his shoulder, so weak, her fingers barely grazed his skin. "Oh, God…I can't breathe."

After brushing a light kiss across her sensitive flesh, he lifted his head and pressed another kiss on her inner thigh. He lowered her leg from his shoulder and leaned back. The want in his face stole what little breath she had left. His eyes were as dark as midnight, his nostrils flaring, his lips damp. He seemed to be having just as much difficulty breathing, his chest rising and falling with the effort.

His gaze drifted from her face to her breasts, and almost as if he couldn't help himself, he touched one, cupping its weight with a reverence that filled her already flushed body with warmth. Her soft whimper brought a new fire to his eyes. She tried to reach for him, wanting to peel off his boxers, but he rolled to his side and stripped them off in one fluid motion.

10

HER GAZE WENT to his cock, which was thick and ready. The tip glistened with moisture. A shiver raced down her back and all the way to her legs. Stretching out beside her, he put an arm around her and drew her to his chest. His erection pulsed against her abdomen. Slipping a hand between them, she wrapped her fingers around the length of smooth, hard flesh. He shuddered, then moved his hips in small thrusts against her palm, groaned and went completely still.

"Not like this," he whispered, forcing her hand away. "I'm too close."

Her brain obviously wasn't functioning yet. She buried her face against his warm musky skin. "So why are we stopping?" she murmured, trying to make sense of things.

"So I can get a grip."

"That's what I'm trying to do."

His gravelly laugh broke off when she touched him again. He briefly tightened his arms around her, kissed her temple, then rose and leaned over her, reaching into the nightstand on her side. He brought out a handful of condoms, some of them falling to the carpet, a couple landing on the bed next to her. He'd managed to hold on to one and lay back while he tore it open.

"Let me." Beth got up on her knees.

Nathan's body was tense and hard, from his well-developed calves to the muscles bunching across his chest and shoulders. He didn't put up a fight. Just let his head fall back on an exhale and handed her the condom.

She couldn't help herself…she had to touch him again. But this time she wanted to know how her lips felt pressed against the smooth hot flesh. She leaned forward and kissed the crown.

His cock jumped.

He brought his head up and his hand shot out to grab her wrist. "Jesus, Bethany. Don't you understand…"

"I know." Quickly she sheathed him.

He'd already curled upright and cupped a hand behind her neck, pulling her toward his mouth. The kiss wasn't gentle. She'd pushed him past patience, maybe beyond his ability to stay in control, and she wasn't sorry. The savage thrust of his tongue past her lips excited her. His fierceness demanded a response; it demanded surrender and filled a deep primitive need she'd never known existed. She should've been wary. She should've wanted him to ease up. But all she wanted was more.

They were both panting when they finally broke apart. He wasted no time sliding his hand between her thighs, probing with his fingers and finding her wet and ready for him. She relaxed her legs and stared up into his face. He was watching her, the hunger in his eyes burning hotter still.

He held her gaze while he eased her legs farther apart and settled between them. Tense as he was, he still took the time to enter her carefully. He was a big man, in every way, and yes, she was ready, but the first breach was still a shock and she jerked. He waited, pushed in a little more and then stopped to brush the back of his hand down her cheek.

She lifted her hips, asking for more, and a faint smile touched the corners of his mouth. He thrust deeper, and when she bucked up to meet him, he pulled her legs around his hips and embedded himself to the hilt. Beth let out a small cry. His answering groan came from somewhere deep in his throat.

He rocked against her, deft, careful movements that she could tell strained his control. She arched into him, knowing exactly what his reaction would be. He began moving, faster and faster, making subtle shifts she knew were designed to learn her body, find the angle that would help her climax again.

It wouldn't take long. His heat enveloped her, igniting a liquid fire that flowed from her belly to her chest and limbs. Feverish and damp, she couldn't take it much longer…that powerful, all-consuming heat.

The burn was becoming too much….

She clenched around him, squeezing, relief almost within her grasp until the force of her climax hit so hard she seized and nearly threw him off.

Finally, finally she felt her body start to float, weightless, like an airy white tendril of smoke drifting up into the clouds. She thought she heard Nathan calling her, his voice a great distance away. Except he was right here, his body hot under her palms.

He let out a hoarse cry and suddenly she was the one hushing him, soothing him, petting his damp feverish skin and pulling him into her arms as his entire body shuddered. He was heavy, pinning her down against the mattress, but she refused to let go. Even when he tried to roll away.

Nathan lifted his head to look at her. She had no idea what she'd been thinking, clinging to him like she was. Embarrassed, she relaxed her arms. He used his elbow to take some of his weight off her and then touched her face with the back of his hand, slowly drawing it down her cheek.

He froze, his brows drawing into a frown. "Are you okay?"

"Yes." She blinked. "Why?" To her sudden horror, she realized she was so full of emotion that her cheeks were damp. She sighed. "I'm exhausted. It feels as if I haven't had a good night's sleep in forever," she said truthfully. "That's all."

He moved completely off her. Before she could roll to the side of the bed, he pulled the covers over them, put his arms around her and brought her to his chest.

It would be crazy to get too comfortable. Insane, she thought as she snuggled against him. Really stupid. She yawned, liking the feel of his soft chest hair against her cheek. Foolish even.

"I should get dressed," she murmured, burrowing in deeper and sighing when he tightened his arms around her.

NATHAN STARED INTO the semidarkness, aware of her soft warm body pressed to his, aware that he hadn't stopped rubbing her arm. And he tried to get a grip on what had just happened.

She'd drugged him. Not literally. But something about Beth's natural scent made him a little crazy. Maybe it was perfume, but he didn't think so. Remembering her fragrance as he'd licked her to orgasm made his whole body tense.

He felt her breath on his chest, shocked that that alone

turned him on, shocked he hadn't dislocated something from coming so hard. "It's still early."

The room was dim, even with both lamps on. He routinely kept it that way unless he couldn't sleep and picked up a book. He had a feeling Beth wouldn't have any trouble drifting off. Her breathing had slowed and it seemed as though she could barely move.

She yawned, the action pushing her breasts against his ribs. Her voice sounded drowsy but her nipples were hard, and his cock stirred. "You still have to take me to my car."

He lightly rested his chin in her hair. "Think you can drive?"

"I don't have much choice."

"Sure you do," he said, without giving the words proper thought.

She lifted her head and blinked at him. "What do you mean?"

"You can sleep and I wake you in an hour." He shrugged. "Or you can spend the night."

"I can't do that." She seemed awake now, pushing away from him and sitting up, her gaze darting around until she found the nightstand clock behind her.

"Fine."

She met his eyes. "But thank you for offering."

He sat up against the padded headboard, raised his arms over his head and stretched. "I didn't want you thinking I was pushing you out the door."

She glanced down at her bare breasts and pulled the sheet up. "I would never think that."

Dammit. It was his fault she felt the need to cover herself. He was acting like a jackass, pretending to be indifferent. "I don't know," he said, his voice coming out too gruff. "Spending the night is probably against the rules."

"What rules?"

"This friends-with-benefits thing." He shook his head. "It's all new to me."

"Well, me, too." She sounded indignant. "I've never been in a situation like this before." She frowned at him. "What?"

He just looked at her, not knowing what to say. Hell, all he'd done was smile.

"You think I make a habit out of sleeping with strange men?"

Nathan winced. They weren't exactly strangers. "Actually, no. If you did, I expect you'd have your pick at the Watering Hole."

"I'll have you know I haven't had sex since moving to Blackfoot Falls. Or for that matter, almost a year before that."

He almost smiled again. "All right, then."

"Okay." She drew in a deep breath and the sheet slipped down a little. Another inch would've made him real happy. Looking confused, she asked, "What exactly are we agreeing on?"

"No rules."

"Oh." She nodded. "I still can't spend the night. On account of Liberty."

"She doesn't know where you are."

"But if I don't come home, she'll assume I had a one-night stand. Sadly, she's too used to that kind of behavior from her mother."

Nathan didn't know what to say. She was looking at him as if she expected him to understand, only he didn't. Not entirely. Beth was an adult. She didn't owe the girl an accounting of her time. "Okay. Smuggling you out of here in the morning wouldn't be easy."

"Oh, God." She pressed a hand to her chest. He noticed her nipples were still hard. In a few minutes he'd be there, too. "I am so not doing the walk of shame. Never have, never will. Especially not in front of your guys," she said, a blush filling her cheeks.

He lounged against the headboard, not bothering to hide his growing arousal under the sheet. "Come here."

A slow smile lifted her lips. "Why?"

"Get over here and find out."

She bit her lower lip, her gaze dropping to his chest, then to his erection. "You're not going to let me take a nap, are you?"

Nathan just smiled.

ALTHOUGH SHE'D HAD very little sleep and not enough coffee, Beth was in a surprisingly good mood as she drove Lib to her penance. At the stop sign, Beth changed radio stations, heard "Rumour Has It" and immediately started singing along with Adele.

"God…" Liberty muttered through gritted teeth, raising splayed fingers to the heavens. "Why are you in such a good mood? It's too freakin' early."

Moving her head from side to side with attitude, Beth pointed to her niece and finished the last few lines of the song before taking her foot off the brake and continuing through the intersection.

Liberty had clapped her hands over her ears. Realizing it was now safe, she lowered them. "You know you can't sing, right? You've been off-key since we left the house."

Beth wasn't sure that was true. Lib was just cranky. She'd been grumbling since Beth woke her up at 8:00 a.m. It was Saturday, so why couldn't she sleep till noon? Why did she have to go to the Lucky 7 on a weekend? She didn't like Woody because he wouldn't let her use her phone and he didn't give her enough breaks…and on and on.

Beth waved to a white-haired man driving past them in a blue Chevy pickup on its last legs.

"Who was that?"

"I don't know." Beth felt her niece's curiosity burning a hole in the side of her head and she glanced at her. "He waved, so I waved back."

Lib frowned. "You got home late last night."

"Yes, I did."

"Where were you?"

"I was with a friend. Besides, I'm not the one on probation, kiddo." Beth turned up the volume and started singing again. Not just because she liked the song. She didn't want Lib asking any more questions.

Yes, Beth knew she was punchy from too little sleep. But the sex had been amazing, so who cared that she hadn't made it home until after 1:30 a.m.? For all Lib knew, Beth had been out dancing. Turned out, Nathan had remarkable stamina. And holy cow, did that man know how to use his tongue.

She kept singing, probably getting most of the words wrong, until Liberty leaned over and turned down the volume.

"If you have to be in a good mood, can't you do it quietly?"

Beth met the girl's glare. "If you have to be a buzzkill, can't you do it quietly?"

Lib gave her another strange look, a mix of annoyance and curiosity. "You're weird."

Beth returned her attention to the road. "Look, I have workers showing up in an hour. You know how much trouble I've had lining up labor," she said. "So, no, driving you today isn't convenient. The least you can do is be civil."

Lib's heavy sigh was the closest thing to an acknowledgment Beth was going to get. That and silence, which was both good and bad. Good because it was easier to daydream about Nathan and everything they'd done last night. Bad for the same reason. She was going to see him in about five minutes. Too late to worry, but she hoped she was a good enough actress and didn't get all giddy and stupid.

The second Beth saw the sun's glare coming off the barn's green roof, her insides started jumping. They were still half a mile away but she slowed the truck when she felt a body flush coming on. The heat surged up from her belly into her chest and neck.

The seductive warmth was like an invitation to flash on last night: Nathan's dark sexy eyes...the lazy, sensual curve of his mouth...him licking his way from her breasts to her...

"Aunt Beth?" Liberty touched her arm. "Are you okay?"

Her foot was on the brake.

Why was the truck in Neutral?

She blinked and looked into her niece's worried blue eyes. "Oh, yeah, fine." Beth pressed a palm to her hot cheek. "Must be getting old. I'm not used to being out so late." She put the truck back in Drive. "That doesn't need to be repeated, by the way."

Liberty grinned. Beth ignored her and drove.

The ranch looked semideserted. As usual, a row of vehicles flanked the bunkhouse and an unattended red ATV was parked outside the barn. A pair of beautiful shiny chestnuts roamed the far back corral. Beth's gaze had immediately gone toward the house. No sign of Nathan, not that she necessarily expected him to suddenly appear, but it was odd seeing no one working with the horses or fiddling with the equipment.

"Woody did tell you to be here by 8:30 a.m., right?" she asked, glancing again toward the house.

"Um, yeah…" Lib paused. "You know what…I think I messed up. He said Monday. Yeah, I'm pretty sure I'm not supposed to be here until Monday."

Beth cut the engine and gave the little opportunist a warning look. Beth knew she hadn't gotten the day wrong, it was the start time she was questioning.

Leaving the keys in the ignition, she opened the door, got out and looked around. An older man holding a steaming mug walked out of the bunkhouse and nodded to her. She didn't recognize him, but she'd ask for Woody if she didn't spot him soon. Past the last corral, two men were coming from the stables. They were too far away to see their faces, but the distinctive bow-legged walk identified Woody. The other man was tall with dark hair, but he wasn't Nathan. She knew because her heart wasn't racing.

She waited for Woody to reach her while she sneaked peeks in the direction of the house. Nathan was probably in his office. Which was good. Better not to see each other right now. That was what she told herself. Disappointment still managed to kick reason in the butt.

"Morning, Woody." She smiled and gave the other man a nod. He returned in kind, then kept walking.

Woody took off his hat and scratched the back of his head, watching sideways as Liberty climbed out of the truck. "How's Miss Grumpy today?"

Beth sighed. "Um…yeah. Sorry. I did speak to her about her attitude."

The older man chuckled. "Don't worry about me. I don't pay her no mind." He stuck his hat back on his head. "She's a bright girl. I reckon she'll figure out the more she grumbles, the more I'm gonna ride her."

"She is bright," Beth said softly, glancing back at her niece, the scowl on her face made worse by the Goth makeup she'd recently adopted. "It breaks my heart."

"Aw, I wouldn't worry about it. She's still wet behind the ears. You shoulda seen Nathan at her age," he said, getting Beth's attention.

She studied the man's weathered face, wondering if he was baiting her. All she saw was kind concern in his eyes. "I can't imagine him being a problem child."

"Nah, nothing like that. But talk about headstrong. I'd swear on my mama's grave that boy knew what he wanted by the time he learned to talk." They both smiled at the exaggeration. "Once he got something in his head, you couldn't convince him otherwise."

Even with what little she knew of Nathan, she could understand what Woody meant. She was so tempted to see what else she could learn, but Liberty was getting restless. "I hope he passed on how much I appreciate you working with Lib," she said in a low voice. "She hasn't had much adult supervision, I'm afraid."

"Well, now she has you, and that makes her pretty darn lucky from what I can see."

Beth was unprepared for the sudden lump in her throat. The sincerity in Woody's voice had gotten to her. She was doing her best, but she just wasn't sure. Sometimes her niece seemed to be getting worse instead of better.

She noticed Liberty moving toward them and asked, "Do you have an idea when I should pick her up? Or do you want to just have her call me?"

"You can't leave me here all day!"

At her raised voice, they both turned.

"Excuse me," Beth drawled the words into a warning.

At the same time Woody pinned Lib with a steely eyed glare and growled, "Watch your tone, missy."

Liberty blinked. For a second she looked startled, then a bit worried. Which was awesome. But she recovered quickly and some of the attitude was back on her face. Though not all, so that was something.

Beth and Woody exchanged private smiles.

"Thank you." Beth started backing toward her truck. "I'll wait for a call." Impulsively she walked over to Liberty, hugged her and kissed her cheek. "I love you, Lib," she whispered. "With all my heart."

The girl's eyes widened, and then she shuttered them and murmured, "Me, too."

"Okay. Call me." Beth saw the faint sheen of tears and quickly stepped away so Lib could regroup.

She hurried to the truck and, as she opened the door, caught Lib furtively dabbing at her eyes. Woody was being terrific. He'd turned his back and was pretending to watch the horses in the corral.

While she regretted making Lib feel awkward, Beth wasn't sorry about the hug. As a child she would've given anything to feel she mattered. She remembered once being told her mom loved her. The words hadn't actually come from Paula herself, but from a kindhearted neighbor who'd found Beth crying and sporting a red welt from the back of her mother's hand. She'd just turned seven but learned quickly to stay clear of her mom whenever a guy dumped her.

As she drove back to the highway, Beth decided she would be more demonstrative with Liberty. And then, without warning, that small child, the one who'd desperately needed a hug all those years ago, wondered if Nathan might be avoiding her.

11

NATHAN STOOD AT the window until the truck disappeared from view. He'd seen Beth hug her niece and sensed the awkwardness between them when the girl dabbed at her eyes and Beth hightailed it to her truck as if she was running from a fire. Damn, he hoped whatever was going on had nothing to do with last night. No reason to think it did, though he'd likely find out soon enough.

His fifth mug of coffee had started to cool, but he chugged it down anyway. He didn't need the caffeine. He was used to not sleeping much. But getting worked up just from looking at a woman? He hadn't experienced that kind of physical craving since he was a teenager. One little taste of Beth was all it had taken to draw him out of hibernation.

Lousy time for him to be having doubts.

Doubts he couldn't ignore, because maybe he'd been wrong about her. Maybe Beth wasn't the type who could handle a relationship based solely on sex. He'd seen her looking toward the house, probably wondering why he hadn't gone outside. That alone wasn't what worried him. Hell, he had no room to talk. He'd been rooted to this vantage point from the moment she'd driven up.

But Beth…she wasn't used to casual sex and she was in a vulnerable place. She had her hands full with her niece. And last night…

Jesus, he hadn't expected last night. His body was already hard. He didn't need to be thinking about how she tasted and smelled or how soft her lips were. The sex had been hot. Hotter than anything he'd ever experienced. Yeah, she knew her way around a man's body, but there'd been those moments of hesitation. She might be more worldly than most women he knew, but she hadn't gotten around as much as he'd assumed.

And he liked that. Call him a pig, but that was the truth. Just listening to her startled gasps and soft moans, feeling her shudder in his arms when he'd slid into her, had pushed him close to climaxing. Didn't hurt that she was tight.

Now so were his jeans.

Shit.

He took the last sip of cold coffee, hoping to blunt his lusty thoughts. The possibility he was fooling himself aside, last night hadn't been just about sex. They'd connected in some way.

Which wasn't part of their understanding.

Watching Liberty trail Woody toward the barn, Nathan let out a long exhale. Between Beth's family issues and renovating the boardinghouse, she had a lot going on. She was under the kind of pressure that could tear down a person's defenses. Or lead to slipping up and being indiscreet. Maybe trying to juggle something outside her comfort zone was just another stressor she couldn't handle.

Hell, he was grateful she wanted to keep quiet about what was going on. Frankly, if not for that, he wouldn't have asked her out at all. He didn't need to be the center of more rumors and gossip.

Nathan rubbed behind his neck. Between the coffee and too much thinking, suddenly he wasn't feeling so hot.

It SEEMED NOTHING in life was simple anymore. Not one blessed thing. Beth had picked up Liberty from the Lucky 7 ten minutes ago. They were almost to town, and Beth told herself she could do this. Get her niece safely home. Strangling the little chatterbox would be in bad form, considering Beth had told her just this morning how much she loved her.

Beth knew it wasn't her niece's fault Nathan hadn't come out to see her. Though she knew he'd been home because Liberty had barely been able to stop talking about him.

Lib turned down the volume and looked at Beth. "Do you know how the Lucky 7 got its name? Nathan explained it to me while he helped me paint."

"No, I don't." She had to be careful and not admit she knew the story. That would require some explaining. "By the way, what happened to calling him Mr. Landers?"

"He told me to call him Nathan. He's really kind of cool," Lib said, her grudging tone indicating she hadn't decided whether to be pleased or feel betrayed. "Okay, so Nathan's grandfather left him and his brothers each seven acres of land for them to do whatever they wanted with it. Nathan knew right away he wanted his own ranch, so he worked odd jobs and saved his money, raised a stallion that ended up making him a lot in stud fees, then he majored in animal science in college—"

The abrupt silence had Beth glancing at the girl. "What's wrong?"

"He kinda slipped and told me something he shouldn't," Lib said. "He asked me not to repeat it."

"I don't think he meant you couldn't tell me."

After another prickly silence Beth again took her eyes from the road to see Lib watching her with open curiosity. And perhaps with a tiny bit of suspicion.

"Why do you say that?" Lib asked, frowning slightly.

"Well, even though I'm not your mother, he knows I'm your aunt and I care about you. And that I'm here hoping to be a stabilizing influence in your life."

"How would he know all that stuff?"

Beth smiled at her. "We had a long talk in his truck, remember?"

She nodded as if everything now made sense and she shouldn't worry.

Beth, on the other hand, felt like a traitor. Or at least the most horrible aunt on the planet. No, she had a right to her privacy, and she had a duty to protect Liberty. It was terrific that she was taking to Nathan. Maybe he'd end up being a positive male figure in her life. "So what did he say?"

Lib muttered a mild curse that Beth decided to let slide. "You can't tell him I told you." She waited for Beth to cross her heart. "Nathan didn't finish college. He left with only one semester to go. And don't worry, he made sure I understood that school is important and I should never think about dropping out."

Beth kept her mouth shut. She wasn't about to weigh in, since she'd also dropped out after two years to work for Fritz.

"Aren't you going to ask me why he did it?"

"Why?"

"He played football and the team was in the locker room when their coach told them a pro scout might be at their next game. Everybody was excited and making jokes about staying in one piece so they'd be able to play. Nathan said it dawned on him that if he got hurt too badly, there went his plans for the Lucky 7. He didn't really need a degree, but he needed a strong back. That was smart of him, don't you think?"

Beth nodded. "He does seem to be successful."

"Yep, and Woody said he was a good football player, too. Good enough he might've gotten picked up by a professional team. But Nathan had always wanted to ranch. Now he's looking into breeding Arabians." Liberty paused, looking pleased with her fountain of information. "He has two already. Ask him to show them to you. They're beautiful. Or I can ask for you. When he gets back."

"Back from where?" The sharply spoken words were out of Beth's mouth before she could stop them. She knew Liberty was staring at her and she avoided her eyes.

"I don't know. A business trip, I think."

"I hope that doesn't mean you can't finish your painting."

"No, I'm supposed to be there on Monday after school."

Beth took a deep breath and nodded at the radio. "Mind turning that up? I like this song."

Liberty cranked up the volume. Too loud for Beth to hear herself think. Not necessarily a bad thing. Inside her head wasn't a fun place to be right now. Why hadn't Nathan mentioned he'd be away? While she didn't expect an itinerary, it would've been nice to know what was happening so she didn't get crazy wondering why he hadn't called.

She sighed. She was being ridiculous. They weren't going steady. They weren't doing anything except having sex. He owed her nothing. Except an orgasm. She had every right to expect that. If they ever got together again.

He hadn't said…
But then, neither had she.

BY LATE MONDAY afternoon, Beth was hanging on to sanity by a thread. The day had started out great. All the scheduled workers had shown up. But then the plumber discovered he'd ordered the wrong pipes, which set him back two days, and three rooms had mysterious electrical problems.

After waiting a week for Mike Burnett to present the bid he'd put together for the carpentry work, Beth had to postpone their meeting so she could provide taxi service for Liberty because Candace had bailed at the last minute.

The good news was that Nathan was expected home in the afternoon. So before returning, Beth had changed from her grubby work clothes to a pair of killer jeans that made her butt look good and a cute Stella McCartney button-down blouse. Rather than go overboard, she chose medium-heel ankle boots.

She did a quick mirror check as she approached the Lucky 7. Her heart rate sped up when she saw a big dark green SUV parked close to the house—the one she'd seen in his garage Friday night. She hoped that meant he was home, and if he didn't come out, she had an excuse ready to justify knocking on the front door.

She didn't see Liberty or Woody as she got out, though she was ten minutes early. Still no sign of Nathan. She rounded the truck bed, too busy admiring a pair of playful roans in the corral to watch where she was going. Her heel sank into something squishy.

Mud. Thick and disgusting. It dragged on her boot when she tried to lift her foot.

Dammit.

She tried very carefully to step backward. And splattered her jeans. Thankfully, she saw a spigot and hose close to the bunkhouse. The jeans would be fine, but not her Italian leather boots if she didn't do something.

It wasn't easy, but she managed to clean them off without adding more mud. But she needed a rag or towel to speed the drying process. She glanced around, looking for someone she knew, and saw Nathan. He was standing about ten yards away, watching her.

Her grip on the hose tightened as if that would slow her pulse rate. "I could use some help here."

For a moment he stayed motionless, then shoved his hands into his pockets and approached...not in any particular hurry. Something about the way he moved unsettled her. Or maybe it was the remote expression on his face. He looked more like the inhospitable man she'd met the first day and not the sexy, generous lover whose bed she'd shared.

He stopped a couple of yards short, training his gaze on her boots. "What happened?"

She blinked at his aloofness. Unless she was mistaken, he was purposely avoiding her eyes. "I didn't see the mud until it was too late."

"What is it you'd like me to do?"

"I need a towel or clean rag so the leather won't stain," she said, his indifference flooring her. What had she done wrong? They hadn't even talked since Friday night.

"I'll ask one of the men to get you a rag," he said, and started toward the barn.

"Nathan?"

He stopped, turned back to her, his brows raised.

"Is something wrong?"

Wariness crossed his face as their gazes met. And for a moment, desire flared in his eyes, burning so hot it made her breath catch. In the next second it was gone, leaving behind a man who looked as if he couldn't be bothered with her. "No."

"Wait," she said when he started walking again. Yes, she was glad he was playing it cool, and she was trying to do the same, but he was taking things a bit far. It wasn't as if anyone was around to hear them. "Can we talk?"

He hesitated. "Maybe later."

Maybe? That made her mad. If she hadn't seen the want in his face it would be different. But after the day she'd had, she could do without the dismissive attitude.

"Nathan?" she called, and this time when he looked at her as if she were an annoying seven-year-old, she raised the hose and sprayed him.

His expression of disbelief was priceless. He glanced down at his jeans and tan shirt. He wasn't all that wet. Mostly his left sleeve and part of his pants leg. He used his dry sleeve to blot his chin.

Oops. She'd gotten him there, too.

Nathan did not look happy. He had no trouble meeting her eyes now.

She stared back, a little surprised herself. She supposed that laughing made it even worse.

His eyes narrowed to a glare. "Are you out of your mind?"

"Yes," she said. "Pretty much."

He brushed ineffectively at his wet sleeve, glanced down at the few damp spots on his boots and shook his head.

"Oh, for heaven's sake, I hardly got you."

Eyeing the hose as if it were a snake about to strike, he said, "Turn that damn thing off."

Maybe she wasn't done with it. "Or what?"

Annoyance shifted to amusement in his dark eyes. "Beth," he said in a quiet, warning tone of voice.

She kept a firm grip on the hose, her finger on the trigger of the nozzle. "Nathan."

He almost smiled as he took a step toward her. "Remember who started this."

"Started what?" Brave words considering there was no escape for her. Ending up in the mud again would really tick her off. Anyway, he was bluffing. What could he do? They were practically out in the open.

That smile, though, she'd never seen it before, and she sure didn't trust it....

From three feet away he lunged for her.

She got off a shot, managing to spray his face before he captured her wrist. In their struggle for control of the hose, he turned the spray on her. Beth let out a shriek. He caught her, his arm tight around her waist, lifting her off the ground. Air left her lungs in a rush, and for a moment she couldn't move or breathe.

"Give up?"

Her back was pressed to his chest, his quick, hard breathing warm on her neck. She'd completely let go of the hose. No water was coming out. She was no longer a threat. Nathan could've safely released her already, except he hadn't.

His arm loosened, allowing her to slide down a few inches. Before she found the ground, he tightened his hold again. Suspended in the air, anchored only by his arm around her ribs, she felt the pressure at the undersides of her breasts. "What do you say, Beth?"

"Fine. You win. Just quit being a damn grouch." She turned her head but couldn't see him. The arm trapping her against him was the one with the wet sleeve. She could feel the moisture soaking into her blouse.

"So if I let you go, you'll behave."

"Don't push it, Landers."

His chuckle stirred her hair and memories of last Friday. "Right," he said, and slowly put her down.

She'd felt his arousal pressed against her backside, and as she turned to face him, she did everything in her power to keep her attention above his waist. A tactical error, as it turned out. She should've avoided his eyes. They told her exactly what he wanted to do to her.

She moistened her suddenly dry lips, drawing his gaze to her mouth. She had to move away from him before one of them did something stupid. If they'd been anywhere else she knew what would happen next. But not here. She stepped back and his hand shot out.

He caught her arm. "Careful."

She looked at the ground behind her. "Thanks," she said, hiding a smile because he was overreacting.

"Aunt Beth, what are you doing?"

Beth jerked a look at her niece. Her eyes were the size of pizzas and her mouth still hadn't closed. She stared at Beth as if she'd just committed treason.

Standing beside her, Woody took off his hat, scratched his head and studied the clear blue sky.

"I was trying to get the mud off my boots," Beth said, and only then did Nathan release her arm.

"Come this way, it's drier." He sounded calm, nothing like the man who a minute ago had eyed her as if she were dinner.

Beth waited for him to give her a wide berth, then walked around the back of the spigot.

"Woody, you mind getting Beth a clean rag?"

He abruptly turned for the barn.

Nathan nodded at Liberty. "I hope you got as much paint on the shed as you did on yourself."

She was still staring at Beth, but gradually dragged her gaze away to look down at the red-splattered denim coveralls Woody had given her. "Oh, yeah," she said, smiling briefly. "Troy pissed me off."

Beth's top, damp from Nathan's wet sleeve, clung to her skin. She plucked at it until she noticed he was trying hard not to watch her and she lowered her hand to her side. "What does that mean?"

Liberty returned her mutinous glare to Beth. "Why are you dressed like that?"

She blinked and glanced down at her designer jeans and the dress boots, suddenly feeling a bit silly. "I'm meeting with Mike Burnett, and I'm late. Is that paint still wet?" She nodded at the coveralls. "I don't want you getting any of that on my upholstery."

Liberty hesitated, apparently decided to accept Beth's explanation, then patted herself down.

Beth chanced a peek at Nathan. He was watching her with a slight frown. She hadn't lied about Mike. She'd postponed the meeting with the carpenter to pick up Lib.

"No, it's dry." The girl looked at Nathan. "Are you going to be here tomorrow?"

"I should, unless something comes up."

"Do you think I could see the Arabians again?" She smiled up at him, tilting her head to the side just a little, just like Candace did when she wanted something from a man.

The image hit Beth hard. Fifteen years old, yet she was already mimicking her mother.

"Sure." He smiled back at her and Liberty practically glowed. "As long as you get your work done first."

"I will." Her gaze swept to Beth, their eyes meeting briefly, though long enough for Beth to get the message.

Earlier Lib had wanted her to see the Arabians, but now she'd purposely been excluded. Her niece had a crush on Nathan. Beth figured it was basically harmless. He was filling the need for an adult male in her life. But it was still a problem. Because it was clear Liberty wanted Nathan all to herself.

THE CRASH ECHOED down the narrow hall. Beth nearly jumped out of her skin. It was more of a booming sound, not shattering glass, so she was moderately relieved. If the guys had dropped one of the new parlor windows she would've had a meltdown. The budget she'd set for the renovation was already becoming a joke.

"Everybody okay?" she called out, interrupting a string of curses that told her nothing. Things could've gone either way. The ensuing silence made her nervous. She set the broom against the wall and made it halfway down the hall before someone answered.

"Yes, ma'am. Just fine." It was the new kid, Duncan. Tall and skinny, he kept bumping his head on the early-1900s doorframes.

She stopped, smoothed her palm over a slight crease in the new drywall while wondering if she really wanted to see the damage. It would only elevate her blood pressure. "Anything I should know about?"

"Everything's okay, Beth." That was Joe. She trusted him. "It's all good."

Now, that phrase she hated. Somehow it always failed to reassure her.

Beth turned around anyway, bypassed the room she'd been sweeping and went to her office. It was already 4:25 p.m. The guys would be knocking off work soon and she'd have to pick up Liberty. After some arm-twisting, Candace had shuttled her from school to the Lucky 7 before leaving for Kalispell. To go to work, or so Candace claimed.

After the hose incident yesterday, Beth had decided

it was best for her to stay away from the ranch as much as possible. She'd been such an idiot, and now she had to be even more careful. In a way, Liberty's crush made everything worse.

Boy, she and Nathan really had to talk. At least he'd tried to get in touch. They'd been playing phone tag today.

Exhausted and tense, Beth sank into her chair, wincing when she hit the busted spring. She understood Lib's need to have a steady, strong male figure in her life. Nathan had been patient and kind with her. Of course she'd grown attached. She barely knew her own father. And obviously he was a terrible role model anyway.

Beth didn't know her own father's name or if she and Candace even shared the same dad. Their mother had refused to tell them. Beth suspected Paula didn't know herself. None of it mattered, not now. But when Beth had been a scared kid, convinced she'd end up alone and homeless, she'd fantasized about having a dad. Someone big and strong, handsome, too, but most of all, in her daydreams, he was kind.

Sighing, she shoved all thoughts of her screwed-up family from her mind. The guys might be leaving soon, but she planned on working late. She'd have to make coffee later. She checked the clock on the microwave.

Sitting on top, the diner's familiar white wrapper caught her attention. Had she forgotten to finish her morning cinnamon roll?

That got her out of her seat. She nuked it for a few seconds, then tore off a hefty piece and stuffed it in her mouth.

"Oh, God." That her sigh interrupted her chewing actually annoyed her. This was crazy. She thought she might seriously be addicted.

Oh, well, there were worse things…

Before she finished swallowing she'd pulled off a second piece. She brought it halfway to her mouth…and saw Nathan standing just outside her door.

He smiled.

She froze, heat filling her cheeks to burning. "How long have— You don't knock?"

"May I come in?"

"Sure, if you wipe that smirk off your face."

His grin remained in place, and like Duncan, Nathan had to duck his head to enter her office. Another two inches and the breadth of his shoulders wouldn't have cleared the door frame, so she couldn't see if anyone was behind him.

God, he looked good.

She gave him a mischievous smile and was about to say something suggestive when a sudden unpleasant thought stopped her cold. "Where's Liberty?"

12

"Woody or Craig will bring her later," he said, not wanting to worry Beth. "I was hoping to get some time alone to talk."

"Oh." Beth let out a breath. "Good."

"Do you have time for me now?" He'd come here to do a lot more than talk. The memory of her body was interfering with his life. Knowing she was so near and not being able to touch her made every day feel like a week. An hour alone with her was all he needed, but clearly he wasn't thinking at all. At the sound of hammers from the other room, he winced. He'd counted on her workers being gone by now.

Hell, him just coming to Blackfoot Falls was reckless enough. Someone was sure to have seen him. He knew better.

"Of course I have time for you," she said. "Please, sit."

He eyed the folding chair. It was old and on the flimsy side. "When do your guys normally clock out?"

"Soon. I can tell them to leave now. They'll still be paid so they won't care."

"No, it's all right." He shoved a hand through his hair, pissed at himself. He was being such a thoughtless jerk.

"I didn't consider the possibility one of them might mention that I was here to Liberty."

"They don't interact with her. Especially now that she's spending her afternoons at your place."

Nathan glanced around the makeshift office. The room was small, yet she'd managed to make the space work for her. A pair of filing cabinets doubled as a counter for the microwave and supply bins. Her desk needed some help, although he doubted the sheet of plywood was permanent.

He spotted what he was looking for…too bad the only other chair was just like the one he was afraid to sit on. Slowly he lowered himself to the metal seat. "I hope this sucker can hold my weight."

"It will," she said, in spite of her nervous expression as she watched him settle in. "I would've offered you my chair, but I busted a spring yesterday so it's not all that comfy."

He smiled at the speck of glaze clinging to the corner of her mouth. He wouldn't tell her. Given the chance, he'd lick it off later.

She narrowed her eyes at him. "Go ahead. Say it."

"What?"

"Why you think I busted a spring. Too many cinnamon rolls?"

He laughed. "Hell, no. I'd never say anything like that. Think I'm stupid?"

Beth did that cute thing with her lips. Not exactly a pout, but sort of.

"I'll tell you what I was thinking. Later. When nobody's around."

Her eyebrows lifted slightly. "I'm sending them home," she said, and got up.

He caught her arm as she came around the desk.

"Yeah, that wouldn't make them wonder what I'm doing here."

"Right." She glanced down at his hand slowly moving up her forearm. "I should give you a tour. You know, show them we have nothing to hide."

"Don't we?"

"You know what I mean."

"For the record, I'm sorry I didn't call ahead." Nathan drew back his hand. "We should have met elsewhere."

Beth stared at him for a moment, then glanced at the open doorway. "I think it'll be fine, so we might as well take that tour."

He got to his feet and followed her out to the hall. Her jeans fit her well, though he doubted any pair could do her justice. The woman had a world-class ass. He knew firsthand, and he'd better stop remembering right now.

"We'll go this way," she said, leading him away from the hammering. "Three of the rooms are almost finished."

"I noticed you've had some roof work done since last week."

"Yes, and the back siding has been replaced."

The narrow doorways and hall, the low ceilings and small windows all spoke to the age of the building. He supposed most people would consider it quaint. Made him feel hemmed in. They couldn't even walk side by side comfortably, which forced him to stay behind her. He wasn't complaining. The mesmerizing sway of her hips kept him plenty occupied, but he still wasn't clear on what they were doing. Whether she was really giving him a tour or trying to get away from the noise and workers at the other end.

Even though she hadn't slowed, he ducked his head for a quick look in a room they were passing. It was tiny, with white walls and a nice wooden floor that needed minimal refinishing. Just like the hall, the room was bare of litter and construction debris.

She was waiting for him just a few feet away. "I know the windows are too small, but I've decided to leave them alone. There's no view from these east rooms, only Main Street. I'm concentrating on the parlor and west room windows since they face the Rockies. Unless it'll be a bigger headache to swap them out later down the road. Any thoughts?"

"Sounds reasonable. What does Mike think?"

She frowned. "Mike?"

Much as Nathan wanted to take back the question, it was too late. What a sorry jackass. The words were already out there. No point in pulling his toe out of the water. "Burnett. Didn't you meet with him last night?"

"Oh, that Mike. He's a finish carpenter. I doubt he'd—" Her brow furrowed, she studied a small spot on the wall, then smoothed her palm over the new drywall. "Huh. You're right. It wouldn't hurt to get his opinion. Mike's smart, and wow, talk about good with his hands. I bet he knows a lot about general construction, too. I'll offer to buy him dinner and see if he won't mind me picking his brain."

Nathan just stared at her as he continued to kick himself. He hadn't behaved this awkwardly since high school. One night of great sex and he'd become a blithering idiot.

Shit.

Hell, if she *was* seeing Burnett, Nathan had no right to complain. Exclusivity wasn't something he could expect. They weren't in a relationship. Far from it. The polar opposite, now that he thought about it. Which sucked...the not being exclusive part anyway.

"Hey," she said. "Come here." She took his hand and tugged him closer. "Feel this."

"What?"

She pressed his palm against the wall. "This shouldn't be there. You feel those bumps?"

Hard to focus on anything but her pink lips and the sweet scent of her skin. But he managed to nod.

"I mean, obviously I know the place is old and I want to maintain the historic feel. Maybe these small imperfections will help…" Her gaze faltered, and she lowered her hand from his.

So it wasn't just him. They were standing too close to each other. Her warm breath hit him where he'd left the top of his shirt unbuttoned. Her body heat seemed to be coming at him in waves, rolling over him, causing all kinds of havoc.

Yet she hadn't moved away. He wasn't sure how much longer he could refrain from kissing her.

Her shoulders lifted in a small shrug and she finally stepped back. "I'll leave the bumps alone. If they bother me too much I'll cover them with pictures."

Forcing his attention back to the wall, he followed the slight ridge with his thumb. He needed the time-out for his damn cock to settle down. "Are there many areas like this?"

She shrugged again. "I noticed one earlier."

"Whoever worked on this should've told you."

"Ideally." Beth sighed. "See, that's the thing. I'm used to a certain level of professionalism that I haven't found in Blackfoot Falls. Let me finish," she said when he smiled. "I'm not being bitchy, really I'm not…"

"I know." He rubbed her arm, then urged her to keep walking farther away from the hammers. "I brought in a general contractor from Kalispell to build my house. Most of the people he subcontracted came with him. Guys around here can be hard workers. But they're ranchers or cowboys. They have a plumbing problem or leaky roof, they patch things up without worrying about making it look pretty."

She stopped at the next room, peeked in and let out an exasperated sigh. Half the walls were covered with red flocked wallpaper. The rest had been stripped, revealing several small holes in the dingy plaster. Looked as if they might've come from bullets.

"This has been my project. Removing wallpaper. I still have four rooms left." She tilted her head to the side. "Maybe I should leave the rest. Just for flavor."

"No." Nathan laughed. Even he knew that red wallpaper was nasty. "I'll help, if you want."

She turned to him, blinking. Puzzled. As if she hadn't understood. "Really? You'd do that?"

"Yes." And dammit, he'd done it again. Acted without thinking. Him helping her strip wallpaper? He could practically hear the gossip now.

"That is so nice." She glanced away before he could tell if the sheen in her eyes meant tears were close behind. "I would never take you up on the offer, so you can relax."

"As long as I'm not causing you grief with your family, I'll be here anytime you need me." He watched her swallow. Hard. As if she had a big lump blocking her throat. He wasn't sure why, though. He wished he could offer more. Even if it meant everyone in two counties speculating about his life, he'd help her if he could. While he still had no desire to feed the local rumor mill, he couldn't let that stop him from trying to make her life a little easier.

He just hoped she wasn't getting weepy.

Anne had cried all the time. Mostly when she'd wanted something. Early on he'd figured out the tears were a form of manipulation. Knowing the cause hadn't changed anything. Either he'd given in to her or walked out of the room, same as always. With Anne, the easy way had been good enough for him.

Beth was different. She was strong and determined, and she stepped up when she was needed. It seemed she kept heaping on responsibility even when she was too weighted down as it was. Now, at least, he understood why. He'd met Candace earlier when she'd dropped off Liberty. It was hard to believe the two women were sisters.

"Nope," Beth said, continuing to walk. "As much as I appreciate you being such a sport, and God help me, I'll probably have to kill myself for turning you down, but this project is completely on me." She stopped again at the end of the hall and gestured through an open doorway. "This is my room."

He looked inside. And deflated like a popped balloon. He'd gotten excited thinking she'd meant a real room, with a real bed. The light green walls looked freshly painted. Modern-style blinds covered the small window. The oak floor was in good condition, but still needed to be refinished.

Yeah, maybe Mike Burnett could take care of that for her.

Like hell.

Nathan's mood started migrating south, but he had to admit, he might need to take a few steps back. Who Beth saw was none of Nathan's business. But if he recalled correctly, Mike was that easygoing guy who'd played baseball in high school and had been popular with the girls. A couple of years younger than Nathan. And hadn't he married Ellen, whose folks owned S & S Cattle Company?

"Come on." Beth was frowning at him. "It's not that bad. Plus, I'm not finished with it."

"What?" He realized he'd been frowning. "No, it's nice. Small, though."

She pointed at the wall. "I'm putting a door there and using the adjoining room as part of my living quarters."

"That'll help." He couldn't see her being happy here in this tiny space with no view. But then he never would've pictured her living in her sister's house. The night he'd dropped off Liberty had been a shocker in more ways than one. 'Course, that made more sense now, what with no beds at all in this place.

"I found an area rug online that I want," she said, smiling, her gaze sweeping over the room. "That's why I went with green walls. I know I did things backward, but it's my house. My room."

Her eyes met his. She seemed genuinely happy. What he'd initially mistaken for pride in her handiwork was simple joy. He smiled back and touched her flushed cheek.

"With that mansion of yours, I know this doesn't seem like much to you…"

"No, that's not—"

She nipped his objection with a finger to his lips, her eyes bright with pleasure. "Run-down as it is, I own this place. It's all mine. No one can take it away from me." Her happiness dimmed, and embarrassment flickered across her face before she turned away. "Acting as my own general contractor is not a mistake I'll be repeating. I had no idea how much work it would be." She shrugged. "I probably shouldn't admit that, since I have my sister and Lib fooled into thinking I'm the smart one in the family."

"Wait," he said when she tried to steer them back toward her office. "I'm not done looking around."

She rolled her eyes, but let him draw her into the room.

"Does the door lock?"

"What?" She pulled her hand from his grasp. "No. Uh-uh. We're not doing that with the guys still here."

"No, we aren't doing *that*," he agreed, and grinned at her glare. "Will we be able to hear someone come down the hall?"

"Normally, yes. Those guys are never quiet. But now? We wouldn't hear a peep because that's the way my life has been going." Her eyes narrowed. "Why?"

He rested his hands on her waist, watched excitement flare in her hazel eyes, then pulled her against him as he lowered his head. Their lips touched. Hers softened under the pressure of his mouth, and she leaned into him, pressing her breasts against his chest.

Too late it registered that he should've waited. A few more minutes and the workers would be gone. He knew he couldn't trust himself around her. That was why he'd taken off on Monday for Butte. He could've seen Tim Wagner's Arabians at the next auction. He'd ended up cutting the trip short because he'd been unable to stay away.

She tasted every bit as sweet as he remembered. Some of it was the cinnamon glaze… The thought made him smile and he drew back to look at her.

Her quiet whimper almost masked the sound of someone approaching.

He released her, and motioned with his eyes toward the door, which they'd neglected to close. She froze, listened to the faint voices, then quickly moved around him to the window and fidgeted with the blinds.

"I'm surprised you didn't choose a room that would give you a view of the Rockies," he said, then tried to clear the hoarseness from his throat.

"I considered it." Beth was quick on the uptake, responding casually. She'd turned in his direction but carefully avoided making eye contact. Her cheeks were still flushed. "I need paying customers more than I want a view. Anyway, I'll be too busy to be hanging out in here much. The bed-and-breakfast concept literally means providing breakfast. Go figure."

"You look thrilled."

"Tickled pink." She shrugged. "Put a gun to my head and I can cook. But baking? I'm hopeless. If Marge can supply enough muffins and rolls, I'll buy them from her. Otherwise, I'll hire someone to handle breakfast. Or maybe I should stick to making the place a no-frills inn. Any thoughts on that?"

"Can't help you there."

Beth glanced past him. "Done for the day?" she asked, and Nathan turned to see a short, stocky guy nod. The young man standing behind him avoided eye contact and stared at his boots.

Nathan thought he recognized him. Earl's son. The kid used to work at his dad's filling station after school. Hard to forget the mop of red hair.

"Have you got a minute?" the shorter one asked Beth, his hands jammed in his jeans' pockets, his shoulders hunched.

"Sure." She studied the guy's somber face. "I'm not going to like this, am I?"

"Probably not."

Nathan had to give her credit. She stayed calm.

"I assume this is a show-and-tell," she said, and got a grim nod. "Let's go." She headed toward the door, then paused to look at Nathan. "Joe, do you know…"

"Hi, Mr. Landers." Joe moved back to give them room. The other kid had disappeared already. "You probably don't remember me. My parents are Preston and Betty."

"Right." The resemblance was there. Joe favored Preston. "Give your dad my best, will you?"

"I'll do that." Joe stepped farther back to let Beth walk ahead of him, but she motioned for him to go first.

She glanced at Nathan before trailing after Joe. If she'd meant to send him a message, Nathan didn't get it. He followed her, trying to decide if he should wait in her office or take off. He'd asked Woody to call him before someone brought Liberty to town, so he wasn't worried about her showing up unexpectedly. But he was uneasy about what might happen after the work crew cleared out.

He couldn't trust himself to keep his hands off Beth.

The whole idea was ridiculous. It was a simple matter of willpower, which normally wasn't a problem for him. If he set his mind on something, it was as good as done. But when it came to Beth, hell, she made everything go haywire. No matter what he did, he thought about her. He couldn't remember ever being this foolish over a woman.

With Anne it had been different. He'd set his sights on her, incorporated her into his life plan, endured a brief snag while he was away at school and then everything had fallen into place on schedule. Anne hadn't been the type to surprise him. At least, not while she'd been alive.

Beth had him so confused, half the time he couldn't tell if he was coming or going.

Like now.

Nathan followed her all the way to the other end of the hall instead of deciding if it was safe to stay.

He hung back, just outside the doorway, eavesdropping while Joe and the redheaded kid explained how the ladder had busted and why there was a hole in the new drywall. It took every bit of his sorry willpower not to jump in and take over for her. These kids might mean well, they might even be hard workers, but they didn't know what the hell they were doing. Beth was clearly in over her head.

She was great, though. She kept her cool, didn't raise her voice, didn't even reprimand them for being careless. He wouldn't have been so understanding with his own men given the same circumstances.

Earl's boy seemed anxious to leave. Not surprising, since his clumsiness had turned out to be the main problem. He gave Nathan a brief, sheepish look as he hurried past him. Next came Joe, who looked depressed.

He gave Nathan a wry smile. "Nice seeing you, Mr. Landers."

Nathan just nodded and watched him shuffle out. Joe had to be at least twenty-one by now, old enough not to be calling him Mr. Landers, but this wasn't the time to mention it.

"Get over it," Beth said with a sigh.

Nathan turned to find her watching him. "Get over what?"

"Joe calling you Mr. Landers. Half these guys call me ma'am." Squeezing her eyes shut, she rubbed her left temple. "It's just plain disrespectful." She looked at him again. "Ma'am? Please. I'm only twenty-nine."

He smiled. "Don't buy another ladder. I'll bring one tomorrow."

"Thanks, but that's all right. I don't need them breaking your things, too." She shrugged. "It's the cost of doing business, as they say."

That cost would soar if she continued to hire amateurs. His cell rang. Woody. Good timing. Nathan didn't need to interfere with Beth's business. He'd known she'd made an emotional decision to renovate the boardinghouse, and that was just one of the things that worried him about her.

Or it would be if this thing between them amounted to anything more than sex.

Speaking of sex…

"You think you might be able to come by the ranch later?"

The disappointment in her face told him straight away that she couldn't. It all boiled down to her being too busy, but he cursed their luck and cursed the fact that she'd awakened the beast inside him. Being numb had been so much easier.

13

"WHERE ARE YOU?" Nathan asked when Beth answered her cell.

The sound of his voice made her smile. It had been a whole week since they'd spent more than five minutes together. "I just got home," she said, pulling the truck to a stop near the back door. The lights were on inside but her sister's beat-up old Mustang was already gone. No surprise there.

"Damn. I was hoping to catch you before you left town."

"Why?" She cut the engine and leaned back against the headrest. "What did you have in mind, cowboy?"

"Meet me at the old line shack and I'll show you."

Beth laughed. "I wish I could," she said, sighing. "I really do." She may not have been with him, but at least they'd started daily phone calls four nights ago.

"I take it Candace isn't there."

"Nope. *Claims* she had to go to work."

"Obviously you don't believe her."

"She's been acting weird. Well, weirder than usual." Beth didn't get it. Candace was never secretive about the men she was seeing, and in fact, tended to brag. Not this time, though. Probably because her man du jour wasn't the same one paying her rent.

"Have you thought any more about this weekend?"

"Are you kidding? It's the only thing that's kept me sane. I told Candace that I'd be away on a shopping trip and she has to stay with Liberty."

"So we're on?"

"Yes, we are." Beth didn't mention her threat to throw out her sister's supply of false eyelashes if she pulled a fast one. Candace might duck out for a few hours, but she wouldn't be gone all night. "We can leave Friday afternoon if you're free."

"What about Liberty? Will she still be working on her art project?"

"She should be done…oh, right." Beth hadn't thought it through. Lib hadn't been to the ranch in two days because of schoolwork, but she'd expect to go there on Saturday. "I don't want her to know we're both out of town."

"I agree. I'll have Woody tell her he's busy this weekend."

"Thanks. For thinking of it." Beth knew it was a mistake to consider Nathan an ally, someone willing to share her burdens. They'd become friends, loosely speaking, but it would be foolish to romanticize his motives.

"You sound beat," he said, his voice a low, soothing murmur that managed to make her feel warm and safe.

"I am. Friday can't come too soon."

"You sure you can't sneak away for a few minutes?"

She laughed. "Only a few, huh?"

"I give a mean back rub."

Beth bit her lip. She knew he meant it. All she had to do was give the word and he'd show up to give her that massage and expect nothing in return. So, okay, he had become a friend. "Lib must've seen me out here, or I'd be tempted…"

"Yeah, I know. It's hard. Maybe I'll stop by the board-inghouse tomorrow."

"Stop by?"

"Yeah…on my way to the Food Mart."

They both laughed.

"Oh, God." Beth saw the front door open. "Here comes search and rescue."

Nathan chuckled. "Go."

She almost told him she missed him, but that seemed over-the-top so she disconnected instead. For a relation-ship that was supposed to be based on sex, they sure weren't having much of it.

LATE FRIDAY, BETH peered through the parlor window, watching Joe and the new guy walk to their trucks. The plumber had already left, so she locked the front door. Old habit. She doubted anyone would break in and con-tinue with the renovation.

She hurried back to her office and checked her phone. No message from Candace, no missed calls. Good.

Most of the day she'd been too busy to feel anxious. She'd even managed to make it through large blocks of time without remembering she was meeting Nathan at 6:00 p.m. But for the past hour she'd been nervous, her stomach jittery.

A packed bag was locked in her truck. All she had to do was drive thirty miles east of town to where Na-than would be waiting. He had a place for her to leave her truck, an enclosed shed, which was perfect, but he hadn't mentioned who owned it.

She'd bet anything it belonged to his family over in the next county. If that were the case, wouldn't it be just peachy if his father or his brothers happened on them skulking around?

See, that was the problem right there, she thought as she let herself out the back and climbed into her truck. Two weeks ago the sneaking around had been somewhat nerve-racking yet exciting. Now it bothered her.

Especially after Marge's visit this afternoon. The diner owner had kindly brought coffee and a couple of donuts, and they'd talked about the construction for a few minutes. It was all very neighborly until Marge had casually mentioned that she'd heard Nathan had been quite…amenable to fixing the lumber situation. The innuendo was clear, and so was the fact that gossip about them had already begun.

She'd been tempted to press Marge for more details, but had managed to roll her eyes and dismiss the whole subject with a remark about people having too much time on their hands.

The question now was, did she mention the incident to Nathan?

Since he didn't seem so touchy lately about people gossiping and she hadn't heard anything from anyone else, including Rachel, who'd stopped by shortly after Marge left, Beth figured she'd keep it to herself for the time being. After reassuring Rachel that the renovations would be done in time for her wedding, Beth had kind of hinted around to see if Rachel had heard anything, but it had been clear she hadn't.

The sun was low, no longer visible but for the orange glow over the Rockies behind her. She hadn't seen another car for the past twenty miles. Any duskier and she might've missed the turn. Her heart kicked into high gear as soon as she saw his green Range Rover parked next to a building she wouldn't have described as a shed. It was as big as a house.

He'd already lifted the garage-style door and motioned for her to drive straight in. Three four-wheelers were parked in the corner, and behind them a large tractor. Other smaller pieces of equipment were stowed neatly along the left wall, but there was still plenty of room for her truck.

She didn't want to block anything and drove in slowly until he signaled for her to stop. After cutting the engine she took a deep breath, anticipation filling her with adrenaline.

Nathan opened her door. "You're right on time."

"No thanks to my motley crew."

Almost before she found her footing, he pulled her into his arms and kissed her. His warm lips gently moved over hers, then brushed the outside corner of her mouth before he slipped inside. Just one slow stroke of his tongue and already she could feel it, the yearning that thrummed through her body, the physical longing, the desperate need for his touch.

She leaned into him, tunneled her fingers through his hair, pressed so close she felt him getting hard, but he wouldn't be rushed. He skimmed a slow hand down her back, used his tongue to make another unhurried sweep of her mouth, keeping to the leisurely pace that felt very intimate, erotic.

She had no defense against this kind of kiss. It made her think too much. Not now, but later, during the alone times in the middle of the night, in her empty bed. If she wasn't careful, she'd start longing for things that weren't part of their unspoken deal.

With a pang of regret, Beth broke the kiss and stepped back. She really wanted to get on the road, drive as far away from town as possible. See if she could shake the edginess.

His eyes were dark, his faint smile full of promise. Oh, yes, he would be doing many delightful things to her in the next two days.

Already she felt better. "We should go. I couldn't stand it if anything ruined this trip."

His gaze narrowed. "Something I should know about?"

"No. Nothing," she said, worrying that it might be a lie. "I'm paranoid, remember?"

The smile was back, and he truly was very handsome. Even with the occasional hint of sadness in his face. But she couldn't think about that because it meant thinking about his late wife as well, and wondering if he'd ever get over Anne.

"Where's your bag?" he asked.

"On the floorboard. Other side." She sucked in a breath when he grazed her beaded left nipple. "I'll get it."

He closed his hand around her upper arm. Just tight enough to send a shiver down to her toes. "Let me."

She nodded, barely capable of doing anything more than walking alongside him. "What is this place?" she asked. "Who owns it?"

"My family. This is Whispering Pines land."

"They won't tow my truck, will they?"

He smiled. "They don't use the shed much this time of year. But I let my brother Clint know we were leaving your truck here."

She would've loved eavesdropping on that conversation, though she doubted he'd told his family about her. Why would he? He got her bag, then gestured her toward his SUV.

"Shouldn't we close up?"

"I will. Let's get you in the Range Rover first. You'll be warmer."

"Oh, I can—" She stopped herself. It was habit to jump in, not just to help, but to take over. She was always the person doing something for someone else...Candace, Liberty and, until a few months ago, her boss and clients. It wouldn't hurt to let Nathan take the reins. "Thank you."

With faint amusement, he walked her to the SUV, stashed her bag in the back and helped her into the brown leather seat, which was heated. Oh, my. Yes, she could get used to this.

A few minutes later they were on the highway headed south. "I don't even know where we're going," she said, startled that she hadn't thought to ask before now.

"I thought we'd stop at a motel about fifty miles from here, if that's all right with you."

"Sure."

"It's nothing fancy, but it's out of the way and only for the night."

"Out of the way works for me. What happens tomorrow night?"

"We head to Missoula. It's a lot bigger than Kalispell so we shouldn't run into anyone. I have a nice hotel in mind and you can do some shopping if you want."

"Oh."

He glanced at her. "You don't sound thrilled."

"No, Missoula will be great. I told my sister I was going shopping, but I honestly hadn't planned on doing any." She sighed. "Though I suppose we can't spend the whole weekend in bed."

Nathan let out a short laugh.

"Okay, that thought shouldn't have made it to my mouth." She tried to think of something clever to add, something that would make him think she was joking, but she was honestly embarrassed.

"For the record, I'd have no problem with that scenario." He found her hand and squeezed it. "You're cold. Feel free to adjust the heat."

Her cell buzzed, and her heart sank like a lead weight.

She saw that it was only Fritz. Thank goodness. "You mind if I take this call? I've been playing phone tag with my former boss."

"No problem."

"Fritz?"

"Is this a trick? Is that you, Bethany? Or your voice mail?"

She laughed. "Hey, don't get your boxers in a twist. I've returned your texts."

"Boxers? Really, darling?" His sigh was dramatic, and she could easily picture his narrow patrician nose stuck in the air. "You've languished in Backwood Falls for too long. You must return to me before it's too late."

"Oh, Fritz, I do miss you," she said, hearing a peal of raucous laughter in the background. "Where are you?"

"Hong Kong."

"What happened to Singapore?"

"I left this morning." Music blared then quickly died, as if Fritz had had someone turn it down. "The royal birthday dinner was a disaster, by the way. A hundred cases of very expensive, very wrong champagne were delivered, and everything went downhill from there."

"Ouch." She cringed. "I'm sorry."

"Oh, well, I suppose I should be grateful that's all that went wrong."

"So you have another job in Hong Kong?"

"No, I decided I deserved a bit of R & R." The music surged again, a horrible frenetic, heavy metal sound, which made no sense. Fritz hated that stuff. He was fastidious in everything from his designer suits to the classical music he preferred. In fact, he hated having downtime, so she wasn't buying the R & R story. "Hold on a moment, would you, darling?"

She glanced at Nathan. His eyes were on the road and she touched his arm to get his attention. "I'm sorry," she whispered. "I won't be long."

"Take your time," he said, reaching over to rub her arm.

His touch was soothing, his large hand remarkably gentle. He was always gentle with her. Fritz would despise the jeans and cowboy boots, but he'd totally swoon over the man. She was halfway there herself.

"I'm back," Fritz said, his words slurred, supporting her suspicion that he might've had one cognac over his limit. Something that rarely happened.

"Where are you? I know Hong Kong…but more specifically?"

"Oh, some club you wouldn't know."

"You don't like going to clubs."

"Quite right, my darling Bethany, but I met the most interesting man on the plane," he said. "I just may take off the rest of the week."

"Oh, Fritz…please, please be careful."

"Aren't I always?"

"Call me again tomorrow, huh?"

He laughed softly. "I will, but I have to go now." He disconnected before she could say goodbye or anything else.

She stared at the phone a moment. They'd forged quite a bond and he understood her decision to quit hadn't been an easy one. Fritz was as much family to her as

Liberty and Candace. And it sure wasn't easy ignoring the guilt she felt for leaving him.

NATHAN HEARD HER deep sigh. He glanced over just as she let her head fall back against the headrest. She'd claimed nothing was going on between her and her former boss, but that wasn't how it sounded. "You okay?"

"Of course." Beth brought her head up and smiled. "I'm here with you and we have a whole weekend ahead of us."

He hadn't expected that response. No drama, just optimism. Nice. "I can't promise to make your problems go away, but I'll do my best to distract you."

"Oh, boy. That's the best offer I've had…well, not ever, but at least since two Fridays ago." She laughed. "I wish I had the guts to turn off my phone. I really do."

"Why can't you? What's the worst that could happen?"

"Well…" She seemed to be giving the idea some consideration. "Liberty might need me."

"Your sister is with her."

"True," Beth said, pausing for a moment. "I love Candace. I really do, but you've met her…she's a complete flake."

A less-flattering description came to mind. He'd never say anything, not his place, but watching her suggestive behavior in front of a red-faced Liberty had pissed him off. "In spite of everything, Liberty seems to have a pretty good head on her shoulders."

"Mostly she does. I can't even explain the graffiti thing. I have a strong suspicion it has to do with an older boy she's been hanging around. Spike's from the city. His father works for the power company and was transferred here."

"Spike?"

"I know." Beth's laugh turned into a groan. "Even worse, he looks like a Spike, kind of Goth and weird. Not to mention he's eighteen going on twelve."

"And Liberty is fifteen? You think they're having sex?"

"No, I really don't. I think they see themselves as kindred spirits—outsiders, misfits." She paused. "You do realize Lib has a crush on you."

"What?" Nathan swung a look at her to see if she was joking. But she looked serious. "No, she doesn't."

"Oh, yes, she does. Why do you think she reacted to us horsing around with the hose last week?"

"Hell, I'm old enough to be her—" The notion of having a teenage daughter stunned him. But it was possible.

"I know," Beth said with a mixture of sympathy and amusement. "Candace is younger than you."

"Fine. But Liberty doesn't have a crush on me. She's interested in the Arabians. We talk. The end."

"I'm not implying her feelings are reciprocated. Jesus." She sighed. "I think it's kind of sweet and I'm glad she looks up to you. She barely knows her father. Sadly, that's not a bad thing. He's a creep. But her feelings for you make *us* even trickier."

Us. Small word, but lots of emphasis. Too bad he couldn't decipher what that meant. Maybe it was best he didn't know.

He noticed oncoming cars stop for a buck and a pair of does crossing the highway up ahead, and he slowed down. Beth leaned forward to watch the deer, an expression of wonder on her face. Even with all she had going on, she knew how to live in the moment. It made him smile. He still wasn't sure he believed Liberty had a crush on him, but then what he knew about teenage girls could fit in his grandma's thimble.

"Your former boss, you seem close to him...."

Beth grinned. "Are you asking if I have a crush on Fritz?"

He shook his head, annoyed with himself. The road was clear now. Traffic was moving again.

"Fritz would have the biggest laugh over that. He'd play up being the mysterious older man in my life. Fritz does love drama," she said. "He's not so much a father figure as a mentor."

"How did you end up in that line of work?"

"Totally by accident. I was in college, working part-time for a catering company Fritz had hired for a client's working retreat. Anyway, I made a crack to another waitress about how stupid it was to serve peas at a business lunch. I didn't know Fritz was behind me and he asked what I meant.

"He nearly gave me a heart attack. I thought for sure I'd be fired and I needed the work. I just told him the truth. Peas roll too easily...as in right off the plate. I saw it happen all the time, so why take a chance? He just smiled, asked if I had a few minutes for him after my shift. He asked some questions...I had commonsense answers and he offered me a job." She shrugged. "I was barely making ends meet, knew I'd have to take a year off school before I could transfer to a university so I said sure...."

"Ever regret not getting a degree?"

"No, not even a little. Fritz gave me an amazing education. I learned so much from him. I even got to see the world."

"You have to miss it."

"I miss *him*. The work was hard and I had no life to speak of, especially since the word *no* isn't in Fritz's vocabulary. He has quite the reputation for achieving the impossible."

"With your help."

"Oh, I played a small part. But he has other staff."

Nathan knew she was being modest. With her take-charge personality and smarts, he had no doubt she'd contributed to her boss's success in a big way.

"Fritz doesn't make friends easily and I worry about him. He needs a confidant, someone he can trust."

"Isn't that you?"

"Well, it was." She smiled. "I guess I still am," she said with a shrug. "But it's different now."

"Still trying to save everyone." The teasing words left him with a bitter taste that surprised him.

"Not anymore." She shook her head. "Just Liberty. Everyone else can fend for themselves."

Nathan let it go. From the beginning he'd figured she'd miss her old lifestyle and eventually leave Blackfoot Falls. Knowing just how close she and her boss were, he could see how it might tempt her. A lot could go wrong with the life she lived now. The boardinghouse wasn't the dream project she'd imagined. Liberty was still getting into trouble at every turn. And she was Candace's daughter, not Beth's—there was only so much influence an aunt could have, no matter how well-meaning.

"How could I have missed that moon?" Beth was leaning forward, gazing at the sky through the windshield. "And all those stars? Nathan, we have to stop."

He took another look at her. "Are you kidding?"

"No. We have to stop. Here. Now. Please."

He wanted to tell her she was nuts, that the same night sky would be there when they reached the motel in fifteen minutes.

Instead, he pulled over to the shoulder. And smiled at the happiness lighting her face, a deep sense of satisfaction growing inside of him. Pleasing Beth had become a daily goal. Listening to her laugh during their phone conversations was like a tonic. But seeing her, knowing he would have her in his arms? Right now he felt like the luckiest guy in the world.

14

BETH OPENED THE door, letting the brisk evening air hit her cheeks. It felt good, but mostly because her face was flushed—for no reason in particular other than that she was happy. God, how much had she missed the clear Montana sky?

"I guess we're getting out," Nathan muttered with a lack of enthusiasm.

"Of course we are," she said, turning to grin at him. "How can you not want to see every star, every constellation—"

"My view is fine from here, where, I might add, it's nice and warm."

"I bet you have a blanket in the back."

He studied her for a moment, as if she'd asked him a trick question. "Bet I don't."

"That's okay." She shrugged. "You don't have to get out. I won't be long."

"Wait. We need to get off the shoulder. I think there's a turnout up ahead."

A mile down the highway they found a spot and she got out. He was right, it was so much warmer in the Range Rover. And she had to pay attention to the uneven ground, a minefield of low-growing scrub brush and tall spindly weeds. She didn't care. Hugging herself, she made it to a small clearing and looked up at the sky.

The sheer number of stars glittering in the darkness stole her breath. She remembered as a kid thinking they had to be magic, that if anyone ever got too close they would disappear.

"Sorry to say I was right…no blanket," Nathan said, coming up behind her. "This should help."

She started to turn, then felt a weight settle on her shoulders. It was his jacket, the warm fleece lining making her sigh with contentment. Then his arms came around her and she leaned back against his strong chest. Her sigh deepened to a moan of pleasure.

"Better?" His quiet murmur glided over the skin near her ear, followed by the light pressure of his lips.

"You're spoiling me," she whispered, tilting her head and exposing the side of her neck to his trail of kisses.

His lips moved down to her shoulder. "Don't set the bar so low."

His heat and scent enveloped her, and she shivered, holding on to his arm—the one pressed across the top of her breasts.

"Are you still cold?"

"No. Different kind of shiver," she said, and laughed. It registered that the arm she was clutching was covered only by his flannel shirtsleeve. "Hey, take your jacket."

She tried to move but he kept her trapped against his body.

"Shh…" He tightened the arm around her waist. "I'm fine." He kissed her jaw. "But you should probably stop wiggling."

"Probably?"

His mouth curved in a smile, the movement slow and

incredibly erotic against her sensitized skin. When he lifted his head, she nearly begged him not to stop. "Are you getting your fill of stars?"

"Never. Look." She leaned back, motioning with her chin. "Do you see Ursa Major?"

"Ah, the Great Bear."

She turned her head to look at him, ridiculously pleased that he recognized the constellation. "It's so cool you know that."

"Don't get too excited. I remember it's part of the Little Dipper and that's about it."

"From school?"

"Camping with my brothers. Seth was into astronomy and used to point out the different constellations. How did you get interested?"

"When I was a kid I would lie on my back in the grass for hours trying to count stars." She returned her gaze to the sky. In another week Ursa Major wouldn't be visible. "I swore I could see patterns beyond the few constellations I already knew and used the library computer to do some poking around."

"You said you grew up in Billings?"

"A few miles north of the city."

"On a ranch?"

"I wish. I wanted a horse so badly I actually had dreams about riding." She hesitated. "I lived in a trailer park when I was a kid…with Candace and my mom, even Liberty until she was three," Beth said, and waited for his reaction.

"You still like horses?" he asked without missing a beat.

She should've known he wouldn't care where she'd come from. "Love them. Rachel McAllister promised to take me riding, though I'm still a beginner."

"I'll take you," he murmured, his arm tightening around her. It wasn't a suggestion. His tone and body language were undeniably possessive. Nathan clearly had decided riding lessons were his job. And while it made her pulse quicken, she wasn't sure how she felt about this subtle shift.

"That might be difficult. You know, with Liberty," she said, watching a cloud pass over the moon. She felt his hot breath on her nape, felt the light graze of stubble near her ear, and she briefly closed her eyes.

"We'll make it work."

"I'll admit, I'm jealous that I haven't seen your Arabians."

"You will." He cupped a breast through her clothes, then circled his thumb over the hardened nipple.

Her breath caught. "Are we crazy for standing out here?"

"Yes." He slid his other hand down to the top of her jeans.

They were tight. He wouldn't get in there without unzipping her, and she hadn't decided if she wanted him to yet. Between the jacket and his body heat, she was pleasantly warm. But he had to be cold.

"We should go," she said, and felt his lips on her neck just as she tried to break away. Oh, they weren't going anywhere soon.

He slid his hand down her tummy, his fingers dipping between her thighs while he rubbed her through the denim.

She was already damp. Could he feel it through the thick fabric? She moved her hips, putting pressure on his erection, and heard his sharp intake of breath. He scraped his teeth over her skin and then caught her earlobe, a gentle pressure that sent shivers racing through her body.

"Nathan," she murmured, her voice reduced to a breathless whisper. "This is nuts. I know it was my idea to stop but—"

The snap on her jeans gave. She gasped at the feel of his palm on her bare belly. The zipper was half-open and he touched her through her damp panties, stroking her while kissing her neck and holding her steady with one arm.

Beth wanted to tell him to wait, even if all they did was make it back to the truck, but all she could manage was a helpless whimper. He kept kissing her, along the line of her jaw, her neck, her shoulder, anywhere his mouth could reach, using his tongue and teeth, yet taking his time until the whole world faded away.

He slipped his fingers inside her panties, and she arched her back, pressing her bottom against his hard cock. Groaning, he plunged a finger inside her.

"I want you," he whispered hoarsely. "I wanted you from the first moment I saw you."

Her knees buckled but he held on to her. "Nathan, please—oh…"

"What, Beth? Tell me what you want."

It wasn't fair…what the vibration of his lips against her skin could do to her. She'd lost track of what she'd been about to say. Something to do with being sensible, about wanting to go find that motel, but she also wanted relief…

From the raw desire spreading through her veins, from the pressure that was building and building…

She tried to squeeze her thighs together. The fever surging through her body was too much. Too fast. Too frightening. Just a bit of relief, that was all she needed. Just so she could think, so she wouldn't completely shatter.

He wasn't having it. His fingers probed deeper and his thumb kept circling…

Suddenly, it was as if the entire sky lit up. Like a hundred lightning flashes. Like the stars had all burst into white-hot flames. She gasped and tried to move away from his hand. Except she was moving against him and he was plunging his fingers faster and deeper. And his thumb…

Oh, God.

It seemed she would never stop convulsing. And when she finally did, Nathan's arm pinning her against him was the only thing keeping her from crumbling to the ground.

After a few moments, she managed to turn around and take his face in her hands. She kissed him hard. He kissed her back until her knees started to buckle again.

"Let's go," he said, his voice rough as sandpaper.

He drew her toward the SUV. Twice they had to stop to retrieve his jacket after it slid from her shoulders, making him cuss and her giggle. Once they were on the highway again, they didn't waste energy talking. Nathan concentrated on driving and they made the rest of the fifteen-minute trip in ten.

The small motel parking lot was mostly empty, and he took the stall in front of number 9, three doors from the office. She waited in the SUV while he checked them in, still in the throes of afterglow. Barely a minute had passed before she saw him headed back toward her. Had he been turned away? Confused, she glanced at the flashing red vacancy sign. Then she saw the plastic key ring in his hand and she climbed out and went around to the back of the Range Rover.

Nathan met her there, but before she could lift the hatch, he grabbed her hand and drew her toward room 9.

"But our bags…"

"Later."

She tried not to laugh when he had trouble inserting the metal key into the lock. "Need help?"

He answered with a glare, then pushed the door open.

Pressing her lips together, she preceded him into a cute, clean room done in rust and tan. "Not bad."

The door didn't *quite* slam.

She turned around when she heard the dead bolt. Nathan was right there, reaching for her, his nostrils flaring, his dark eyes fierce and hungry. He caught her shoulders and pulled her toward him, letting his hands slide down her arms as he kissed her. She wasn't fooled by his restraint, by the hands loosely cupping her elbows. He'd said he wanted her, and she could feel every tension-riddled ounce of that desire radiating from his body.

He deepened the kiss, and when he lowered his hands, she looped her arms around his neck. He went for the zipper of her jeans, then yanked them down and off with a swiftness that left her stunned and breathless. It took him only seconds to strip off the rest of her clothes, less than a minute to get rid of his...boots included.

They yanked the covers back together. He had a condom out before she'd crawled between the sheets.

"What do you think you're doing?" he asked, a faintly amused smile tugging at his mouth.

"What?" She eyed his erection and felt her heart thump as she pulled the sheet up to her breasts. Good thing he was already tearing a foil packet open. "You prefer to go back outside?"

"What I prefer," he said, "is to see you." He jerked the sheet out of her hand.

Laughing, she tried to snatch it back. But he'd already sent it sailing to the foot of the bed.

"That's better." He ran his gaze down her body, and she watched his cock twitch.

"Don't put the condom on yet." She lifted her gaze to his face. "Please."

"Beth…" He let out a shaky breath. "I'm not going to last."

"I know. Just for a minute." She extended a hand, wanting him closer, and when he hesitated, she gave him a seductive smile and lightly pinched her left nipple.

"Dammit," he muttered, crawling beside her, only to stroke his tongue up her breast until she moved her hand.

She cried out when he clamped his teeth around the nipple she'd used to taunt him. Not hard, just enough to make his point. He started to suckle her but she shoved him away.

"Lie back," she ordered.

"Bethany," he drawled, his voice a low, rough growl. "Bad idea."

"You don't know what I'm going to do."

"I think I do."

She just smiled and pushed him onto his back.

Reaching behind his head, he adjusted the pillow. The way his biceps flexed made her swallow. When she moved down to his aroused cock, her mouth went so dry another swallow wasn't an option. "What ever happened to 'no means no'?"

"Seriously?" She shifted her gaze to his face. "You really don't want me to…?"

His expression torn, he sighed. "Well, damn."

"That's what I thought," she said, and leaned over, bracing a hand on his hard-ridged belly, then licking the silky head of his cock.

Nathan shuddered even before she took him into her mouth. She slid her lips halfway down, felt the tension pulsing through his body, felt the straining muscles beneath her palm. She slid her mouth down as far as she could, then back up, then sucked lightly. Groaning, he curled his fingers around her arm.

She didn't think he necessarily wanted her to stop, but she lifted her head and looked at him. "What do you want, Nathan?"

He locked gazes with her and tugged her arm, bringing her face closer to his. "To be inside you," he murmured, his voice low and mesmerizing, his lips lifting in a faint but self-assured smile. "And a rain check."

Their mouths met, open and hungry, her breasts pressed against his muscled chest, the soft yet crisp hair tickling her nipples every time she tried to take a breath. She didn't know how he'd managed it so quickly, but he was already slipping on a condom.

Her skin tingled. Everywhere. Places he hadn't touched yet. Places that shouldn't tingle at all.

He took hold of her hips and lifted her until she straddled him. She bent to kiss him, parting her lips for his hot, demanding tongue as she reached between them and positioned him against her, then slid down. All the way.

Letting out a harsh breath, he froze. "Jesus," he murmured. His shoulders, his chest, his whole body trembled. He squeezed her hips; the pressure of his fingers digging into her flesh was almost too much, but then he loosened his grip.

Beth lifted up, and he bucked up to stay with her. He moved his hands and closed them over her breasts. The rough texture of his work-hardened palms against her tender flesh made her quake, made her clench. His head went back. He shut his eyes and groaned.

She splayed her hands on his chest and rocked against

him. Slowly, finding a steady rhythm, seeking that perfect angle that would drive them both crazy.

Nathan opened his eyes, barely; his lids seemed too heavy to lift all the way. But the smile was back…a little feral, a little arrogant. "You're killing me."

"Well, now, that wouldn't work out for either of us," she said, and imagined *her* smile was a bit haughty, as well.

The right corner of his mouth hiked a tad higher. But he just watched her, his slitted eyes giving nothing away while he gently kneaded her breasts. She kept rocking, one time leaning forward far enough to take a nip at his chin. His expression didn't change, but she wasn't fooled. He was up to something. This time when she rocked back, she arched as far as possible, giving him quite a view.

The noise he made sounded as if it came from a wild animal. Just as she moved to center position, he thrust up into her and she almost lost her balance. She'd thought she'd taken him in all the way. She was wrong. Very wrong. Another thrust and she had to cover her mouth to keep from being too loud.

His arms came around her, and hugging her to his chest, he turned them over so she was on her back. He pushed in so hard she slapped at the pillows and mattress, looking for something to hold on to. Nathan touched her face. "You okay?"

She nodded and held her breath. Again, he came in hard, stretching her to her limit. It seemed as though he was barely moving. And yet the short, deep thrusts were pushing her closer and closer to the edge.

"God, Beth, you feel so good." His raspy murmur glided across her cheeks and lips. "I can't hold off any—" He kissed her hard then buried himself so deep it left her breathless.

His hands were braced on either side of her, his arms straining, his head thrown back. He kept moving inside her, longer than she'd expected, his chest heaving from the violence of his climax.

Her body flushed hot, blazing hot, and she started to spasm. She squirmed beneath him, the searing heat threatening to torch them both. He slowly brought his chin down and looked at her, watched her shatter into a million tiny pieces. The tenderness in his eyes as they convulsed against each other made it impossible for her to swallow.

No man had ever…

It was the climax, she told herself, and closed her eyes, waiting for her body to calm down.

A second after the last spasm died, he touched her cheek.

Like a coward, Beth kept her eyes shut tight.

15

THE INSTANT NATHAN noticed the estate-sale sign, he squeezed the hand he'd rested on her thigh, hoping to distract her.

"Oh, look. Another one. Wow, we've really hit the jackpot today."

Sighing, he moved his hand back to the steering wheel so he could make the turn. No use arguing with her. Even if he couldn't stomach one more garage packed with junk, he wouldn't try to talk her out of it. She'd looked so happy poking around all the weird items people were trying to sell. He suspected it had less to do with a desire to shop and more to do with getting away from the boarding-house and her sister.

"I heard that sigh and I don't feel bad. Not one bit." She grinned. "This was your idea."

"To stop at the first one, yeah. Five hours ago."

"Look on the bright side. The last two were yard sales, this says estate. Maybe the stuff will be better."

Yeah, he wasn't buying it. They'd already been to both, and the only difference he'd noticed was the size of the garages.

"Okay, this is the last one, I promise." She leaned

across the console and kissed his cheek. "And I'll make it up to you."

That got his attention. He made the turn, then slid her a smile. Her bottom lip was still slightly puffy from a few hard kisses. He felt like shit about that. "You know I'm teasing. I don't mind stopping. You did find the ottoman and a couple of nice prints for your lobby."

Frowning, she shrank back to her side. "Don't worry about my lip. It's fine."

He found the house hosting the sale, pulled the SUV behind two parked cars and cut the engine. "I am sorry I was rough with you. It won't happen again. But that's not why I said I don't mind stopping."

She glanced down at her hands, then out her window. Almost as if she didn't want to meet his eyes.

"Beth? What's wrong?"

"Nothing." She rubbed her temple. Neither of them had gotten much sleep. "You weren't rough with me. We were in the moment. Are we supposed to hold back? Tell me if the rules have changed." She glanced at him. "Oh, God, I'm sorry. You're being so great and I'm being crabby. But it has nothing to do with you."

"Want to talk about it?" Did *he?* Nathan wasn't so sure he did. But then, lack of communication had been one of the problems with his marriage. "It might make you feel better."

"Maybe. You know what…I think I'm done." She looked toward the modest brick house. An elderly man standing outside the open garage waved to them. Beth sighed and waved back. "I would feel awful driving away now, but this is the last one."

"Not on my account, I hope."

Shaking her head, she opened her door. "Let's go see what treasures await us."

He smiled, got out and followed her up the short driveway. She seemed to be in a better mood, but something had gotten her down. Whatever the problem, if it helped her to talk about it, he'd listen. In fact, he wanted to be her sounding board. That would shock anyone who knew him. But this new attitude wasn't about him. He hadn't suddenly undergone a personality overhaul. This was about Beth and giving her an opportunity to vent.

"Afternoon, folks." The man's hands were stuffed deep in the pockets of his baggy overalls and he wore a wool cap over tufts of white hair, though the temperature was mild. "My name's Albert if you have any questions. There's furniture for sale inside if that's what you're looking for." He nodded at the door to the house. "Everything's marked with price stickers."

"Thank you," Beth said, glancing around at the folding tables covered with tools, Christmas decorations, small appliances and knickknacks that were being ruthlessly pawed through by a middle-aged woman with a small child tugging on her shirt. "I would love to see the furniture, if you don't mind."

"'Course I don't. I can't sell anything I'm not willing to show, now, can I?" The old-timer's faded blue eyes lit with humor. "You go right on in. I'll check with you in a minute."

"Nathan?" She glanced back at him. "Do you want to come? If not, it's okay."

"I'm right behind you."

Albert grinned at him. "You have a real pretty wife, son," he said in a hushed voice. "She's got a good aura around her. That comes from a kind heart."

At first Nathan thought he'd misheard, realized he hadn't and held in a laugh. Albert in his farmer's overalls and the word *aura* were hard to reconcile. "Yes, she does."

Beth had already disappeared inside, and Nathan found her in a small living room crowded with an odd mix of antique tables and cheap department-store chairs, with a lifetime of framed memories hanging on the walls. Crouching to examine what looked to be a hand-carved oak table, she slowly skimmed her palm over the smooth wood with the reverence it deserved.

Even from where he stood, he could tell it was a fine piece. Probably passed down through the generations. He doubted it was for sale, though who knew why people wanted to let things go.

Beth looked up. "It has a sticker," she said with quiet awe. "And it's priced too low. I don't understand why he's selling this table at all."

Her troubled gaze flicked to the other side of the faded orange couch. "That one, too. They're both antique, right? We have to tell him. I can't imagine anyone being willing to part with these."

This wasn't the first time she'd surprised him today. He would've guessed her taste to be more sophisticated. But it was the older handcrafted items that drew her.

He offered her a hand as she rose. "He might need the money, or maybe he's moving," Nathan said, then noticed the bronze urn sitting on the mantel. "Or maybe his wife passed away…."

Beth met his gaze.

Voices carried from the back of the house and they both turned toward the narrow hall.

"Got more furniture in the bedrooms." Albert appeared from the opposite direction. "Some folks are back there now." His gaze dropped to the table Beth had been admiring, and he gave her an approving smile. "I figured that might interest you."

She blinked in surprise. "Um, Albert—"

The voices were coming toward them.

Nathan put an arm around her shoulders. "We'll take both tables," he said, and the old man nodded as if he'd already known it was a done deal.

"But, Nathan—"

He gave her a squeeze and lightly kissed her lips. She frowned, but he saw in her eyes that she'd gotten the message.

"Go have a look in the back," Albert said, carefully peeling off a sticker, a hand tremor making the task difficult. "My Ida, may God rest her soul, her great granddad carved both headboards out of cherry. Took him four winters, the way I heard it."

"Thank you." Nathan drew her toward the hall, then stepped aside to allow the young couple with the loud voices to pass.

After exchanging nods and smiles, Nathan took Beth's hand and led her to the first open door.

"We're shopping for something more modern," they heard the woman tell Albert. "But thanks for letting us look."

The moment they entered the room, Beth started to say something but was distracted by the headboard. It was a beauty.

The intricate patterns had required a patient hand.

"This is stunning." Beth moved in for a closer inspection. She traced two evenly matched scrolls with her fingertips.

"My parents inherited several handmade pieces from my mom's family. Some really nice stuff," Nathan said. "But this work is in a class by itself."

"That's why—" she glanced at the door and lowered her voice "—I can't buy any of this furniture, and we have to convince him to not sell it to anyone else."

Nathan hated the misery in her face. "He's a grown man."

"You heard him, he lost his wife. Maybe he's still grieving. These are family heirlooms. Later he'll regret selling things she cared about. You of all people should understand." She paused and stared down at the floor. "I hope that didn't sound insensitive."

"Not at all." Nathan put his hands on her shoulders and waited for her to look at him. "I've left the house the way it is out of indifference. That's it."

Confusion darkened Beth's eyes. He could see it was past time for them to have a talk. But it wouldn't be here. "People mourn and react in many different ways and for reasons most folks will never understand."

Beth slowly nodded. "What if he's a bit senile? He might have children. I wonder if they know what he's doing."

"He seems to have his wits about him." Nathan massaged her tense shoulders while she bit at her lip. "Beth." He nudged her chin up. "Sweetheart, you need to leave this alone."

"If it's about money, I could pay him the sticker price and leave the tables as a gift…."

"And rob the man of his dignity?"

Her lips parted with a soft sound of distress.

Nathan sighed and rubbed his hands down her arms. "Tell you what…we'll let him know we think the prices are too low and we want to give him an amount we can live with. How's that?"

She didn't seem convinced that was the best solution

but she finally nodded. "I'll leave my phone number, too. In case he changes his mind."

He agreed, though he was pretty sure that would never happen. "What about the headboard and nightstand?"

"No." She stepped back, glaring at him as if he'd suggested stealing the furniture. "I feel horrible as it is."

"All right. But remember, if not us, someone else could come in and offer him peanuts for everything."

"True." She gazed longingly at the headboard. "Honestly, I doubt I can squeeze much more out of my budget."

"Let me buy them for you," he said, and stopped talking when he saw fire in her narrowed gaze.

"And rob me of my dignity?"

"Jesus." He pushed a hand through his hair. "Seriously? You're going to use that?" He had to laugh, even though she obviously found no humor in the exchange.

"How are you folks doing?" Albert strolled in, hands tucked in his pockets again. "You make it to the other room yet?"

"I still haven't recovered from this headboard," Beth said. "Your furniture is stunning."

"Let's talk turkey, Albert," Nathan said. "We want everything, tables, headboards, nightstands, and we're willing to triple the price so we can sleep with a clear conscience."

Albert chuckled.

Beth tugged on Nathan's arm. "Excuse me, may I have a word with you in private?"

He ignored her. "I'll have to give you a personal check, but we'd leave everything here until I bring a truck back. Though we could take the two tables with us now, if that's not a problem."

"None at all, so long as we can agree on the price.

Heck, a fella showed up at the crack of dawn and offered me four times what I'm asking. I didn't care for him at all. You write that check for what's on the stickers and we have us a deal." The elderly man didn't offer a hand-shake, and Nathan left it at that.

"Albert?" Beth began softly. "Do you understand this headboard and everything else are worth more than—"

"Your husband and I already have a deal."

"Oh, he's not my husband," she said, looking startled. "We're friends."

Albert frowned at Nathan. "Here I pegged you for a smart man. Better hurry up and marry this woman, son. You'll be darned shocked at how fast life slips by you." With that he turned and walked down the hall toward the living room.

They followed him to the rickety kitchen table, and Nathan wrote a check for the exact figure Albert gave him—an amount that included the unseen furniture in the second bedroom. Beth stood by without saying much, until she asked Albert for a piece of paper and wrote down her phone number.

He'd never call, certainly not to reclaim the furniture. Nathan had a feeling the old man had known the moment he'd seen Beth that he wanted her to have everything. A younger Albert, along with a smiling woman and two happy children, occupied most of the pictures hanging on the walls on each side of the fireplace.

And three urns sat on the mantel.

The old man's coveralls weren't just baggy. They'd once fit the younger, robust man in the family photos. Albert was sick. He hadn't said, though he'd quietly told Nathan to be sure to pick up everything within ten days. Nathan saw no reason to share his observations with

Beth. It would only upset her. That, and he was reasonably certain Albert preferred she remember him as the grinning old man she'd made blush with a goodbye kiss on the cheek.

THIRTY MILES TO Blackfoot Falls. Beth yawned as she read the sign. She wasn't ready to go home yet. Two days and two nights hadn't been enough time. She didn't care that they hadn't made it to Missoula. After shopping on Saturday, they'd checked in to the first motel they saw and stayed in for the whole night.

Admittedly, she was a little sore from too much physical activity, but she had no complaints. Her only objection was that she didn't know when she'd be able to see Nathan again.

Almost on cue, he reached for her hand. "Any chance you can call your sister, check on Liberty and tell them you'll be home in the morning?"

"Where would we go?"

"My house. I can take you to your truck before daybreak."

"It's tempting…" She thought of all the loot stashed in the back. Of course, Albert's tables came to mind first—she still hadn't made peace with the purchase. But at least she had proof of a shopping trip if Liberty got nosy. "I'll give it a try."

Candace didn't pick up, and Beth didn't bother leaving a message. Instead, she called Liberty and found out her mother had left an hour ago and would be gone for two days. What the hell was Candace up to? She'd been disappearing too much lately. Beth just looked at Nathan. He'd heard enough to know it was a no-go.

"That sucks."

Coming out of his mouth, the words made her laugh.

She liked when he surprised her in little unexpected ways. Although yesterday, when he'd mentioned being indifferent to the decor of his house, that had tipped the scale toward shock. He hadn't said a word about Anne since, and she resisted asking, not willing to ruin their weekend.

"Let's not end today on a downer," he said. "Tell me where you're going to put your tables."

"For now, I'll keep them locked in my office. But eventually they'll go in the parlor." Brave of him to bring up the topic. They'd had a few heated words when he'd tried to refuse her check for her share. Then she'd threatened him if he didn't cash it. "When are you picking up your headboards and nightstands?"

He gave her a wry smile. "The end of the week."

Noting that he hadn't suggested she go with him, she wished she'd phrased the question differently. She knew he wanted her to have the furniture. But she wouldn't accept such a lavish gift from him, or any man.

"Nathan? I want to ask you something that's none of my business, so feel free to brush me off. It's about Anne."

He nodded as if he'd been waiting for the question. "You're referring to what I said yesterday."

"Yes." Beth stared closely at him, not sure what to think since she'd expected an opposite reaction. He seemed fine.

"I'd known Anne since we were kids. Not well, since she was two years younger. Growing up in the same small town, you know how it is. The spark wasn't there until I was a senior. Then we hit it off in a big way. I didn't look at another girl, even after I left for college. Anne was everything I'd wanted...." His mouth tightened for a moment. "That's what I thought, but I was still a kid. She knew I was determined to start the Lucky 7—we talked about it all the time. She seemed excited. I assumed we'd get married someday.

"After high school she went to a community college in Kalispell. The first year was kind of rocky for us. I was playing football to keep my scholarship, so I couldn't come home much during the season. She was involved with her school's drama department. We broke it off for a few months, got back together, split up again. Then, out of the blue, she called me one day, said she'd made a mistake and she wanted to build the Lucky 7 with me.

"Hell, I was happy. We went back to the way things were until I quit school. I came back, worked like a dog to get the ranch started while she stayed in college for another year, but we saw each other a lot. As soon as the Lucky 7 started making money, we got married. I assumed we were doing great. We'd even decided to start a family...."

Hands tightening on the steering wheel, he exhaled. "I found out that I didn't know Anne as well as I thought. The night of the accident, she and her friend Bella were on their way to Kalispell to audition for a play. I was away at a cattle auction and had no idea she was gone." He shrugged. "Turned out every time I left town she'd take off for one audition or another. According to Bella, Anne had always wanted to be on the stage. She'd never said a word to me. I mean, I knew she'd liked drama class in high school...."

Nathan shook his head. "Since we'd agreed to pump extra cash back into the business, it took a while to finish the house. Once we'd made it over the hump and were flush, she was excited about decorating and ordering furniture. I thought everything was fine. But our marriage was a lie. She wasn't happy. And I was too damned invested in the ranch to notice."

Not knowing what to say, Beth hesitated. She knew what she *wanted* to ask him, but was it the right thing? Oh, what the hell…. "Were *you?*" she asked, and he frowned. "Were you happy?"

His head reared back. He looked as though she'd completely stumped him. She wasn't surprised. Nathan would feel it was his responsibility to take care of his wife, be the provider.

"Yeah…I guess," he said finally. "I'd always hoped she'd be more of a partner in making ranch decisions. But I'm sure she had a whole wish list of things I could've done better." He sighed. "What I can't let go of is that for two years she let me believe we were trying to have a baby. After the funeral I found her birth control pills."

He looked at Beth, but quickly turned his gaze back to the road. "That was bad enough, but not a week later I discovered that practically everyone knew Anne wanted to be an actress. That she used to go off to auditions and God knows what else every time she could."

A gasp escaped Beth's lips. She could almost see the anger and hurt weighing down his shoulders.

"Still, it was my own damn fault. I should have known. Should have seen the truth for myself."

There was nothing Beth could say that would help. After that first night with him, she remembered wondering whether he would ever get over his wife. Now she wondered if he could ever trust a woman or himself again.

16

On Saturday, when Beth arrived at the Lucky 7 to collect Liberty, Nathan and his brother were in front of the house, talking.

Nathan had told her Clint was going to help him pick up the furniture from Albert, but she'd assumed he'd have gone home this late in the afternoon.

She smiled as she stepped out of the car, but couldn't help stealing a glance at the barn. Today was Liberty's last day of penance, no more drop-offs and pick-ups, and Beth didn't need a parting incident to set her niece off.

With mixed feelings about meeting Clint, Beth slowly approached. He knew she and Nathan had gone away together last weekend. Beyond that, she had no clue what Nathan might have confided in him.

"Perfect timing," Nathan said, and for a scary moment she thought he was going to put his arm around her. Instead, he gestured to his brother. "I wanted you to meet Clint."

"Hi," Beth said, extending her hand.

"I'm really glad to meet you," he said, the sincerity in his smile and eyes matching his firm handshake. "I've heard a lot about you, Beth."

"Really?" She shot a wary look at Nathan. The way he was looking back at her… God, she could scarcely breathe. Even someone who didn't know him as well as his brother could have seen there was something going on. "Yes, I'm sure you've heard about my niece terrorizing him."

Clint just grinned. He had the same dark hair as Nathan and his eyes were brown, too, but lighter. The smile was different, though. "I gotta get back and help Dad move hay. But I hope to see you real soon," he said to Beth, and then exchanged a cryptic glance with Nathan. "Come to Dad's birthday dinner, bro. Make Mom happy…Dad and Grandma, too. And think about what I said."

"Sorry if I chased him off," Beth said as she watched him walk to his truck.

"No, he really did have to go. He only hung around to meet you."

"Why?" she asked, facing Nathan. "What did you tell him about me?"

After a second's hesitation, he said, "The truth."

She let out a soft gasp. "That we're friends with benefits?"

"No." He bit off the word and stared at her as if she'd insulted him.

Beth sighed. Of course he wouldn't tell his brother or anyone else. That was private.

"The birthday dinner for my dad that Clint mentioned… you want to go?" Nathan asked, watching her closely.

"I don't know. I—where? When?" It didn't matter. She was stalling until she recovered from the shock. He wanted her to meet his folks?

"At their place. Next Wednesday. It'll be small, just the immediate family."

"Um, wouldn't that be awkward?" She glanced over her shoulder and saw Liberty and Woody, still a ways off, loaded with paint supplies and heading toward the barn.

"If I thought so, I wouldn't have asked." He sounded tired. She turned back to him and saw the weariness in his eyes. "Think it over. We should also consider including Liberty."

She gaped at him. "Why? Because today is her last day? Nothing's changed. She's told me you and Woody said she's welcome to come back anytime, which I appreciate—"

"Is that what's stopping you from telling her about us?"

The question took her by surprise. Yes, their relationship had been evolving into something more intimate, at least in her mind. But they hadn't discussed it. "What do you mean by 'us'?" she asked, and waited, letting the silence stretch until it nearly snapped. "We're friends who have sex…is that something I should explain to my fifteen-year-old niece?"

She noted the sudden tightening of his mouth, but she didn't regret speaking candidly. If she was upset, it was with herself for foolishly hoping he'd suddenly blurt a confession that he cared for her.

But he just studied her for a long, uncomfortable moment, then stared off in the direction of Lib and Woody.

Dammit, she wished they hadn't broached the subject now. Not out here where she couldn't touch him. "You know, it wouldn't be a bad idea," she said with a teasing smile. "Letting Lib meet your brothers. Maybe she'd transfer her crush to one of them."

He gave her a faint smile. "Am I that easy to replace?"

"No." She shook her head, horrified at the surge of emotion that blocked her throat. She'd entered their arrangement confident that good sex was all that mattered. Building a friendship would be a bonus. But they'd already passed that point…at least she had. "I'll talk to Liberty," Beth said. "About going to dinner."

Nathan nodded and flexed his hands. She knew he wanted to touch her, just as she wanted to touch him. But they couldn't. "Liberty is on her way over here. If dinner doesn't work out, no sweat, okay? I don't want it causing problems—"

The way he cut off the sentence bothered her. Maybe he was having second thoughts about going so public? "I'll call you later."

"Any chance I'll see you tonight?" he asked.

"I hope so." She glanced over her shoulder and waved to Liberty, wishing they could talk now. "I want to make sure Candace will be home."

Nathan abruptly changed the subject to the Arabians, and seconds later Liberty joined in the conversation. Beth mostly stayed quiet, observing and listening. She liked seeing the passion in Liberty's eyes, discovering how much she'd learned from Nathan. They had forged quite a bond. And when was the last time she'd seen Lib this happy?

Beth prayed she'd stay that way.

NATHAN LISTENED TO Big John's concern about why the hay in the east barn should be moved, but he was aware the second Beth's truck disappeared from view. He wasn't sorry their conversation had been interrupted. Nathan didn't think he could've stood another minute of watching Beth slowly withdraw from him. Sure, he knew her silence had been intended to give Liberty the floor, but there was more to it.

He was beginning to read Beth pretty well. Too often

they only had time for a quick lunch in her office, a cup of coffee here and there, a few kisses, but the late-night phone conversations? He'd never done so much talking in his entire life. And one thing was perfectly clear to him—Beth would do anything to protect Liberty. Even if it meant cutting ties with him.

While he admired her loyalty and commitment, he doubted her ability to rationally assess the situation. Liberty was still a kid. He didn't know anything about young girls' crushes, but he knew kids had short attention spans, and that Liberty was more interested in the Arabians than anything else.

Dammit, what was he supposed to do? Discourage Liberty from hanging out with him? Stop seeing Beth before things went too far?

He was as surprised as anyone that he'd told his brother about Beth. That he was considering letting Liberty in on their secret. Now he kicked himself for even mentioning the party. What if they let the cat out of the bag and Beth decided she couldn't handle it? It hurt like hell knowing she might kick him to the side instead of looking for another solution.

If all they had between them was sex, he wouldn't blame her for ending things. But their relationship had crossed over to something more intimate a while ago. He felt certain she could see that, too. Neither of them had said anything, but their feelings were as clear as day, so what was there to discuss?

Maybe he was worried for nothing.

Or just maybe the situation with Candace had Beth thinking about leaving Blackfoot Falls and taking Liberty with her. The way she cared about her niece, if she thought it necessary, even having all her money tied up with the boardinghouse wouldn't be enough to keep her here.

And neither would he.

"Well, don't you look as happy as a pig being dragged away from a feed trough." Woody took off his hat, glanced toward the road and scratched his head. "Want to tell me what's going on? Big John thinks you've gone loco. I might have to agree."

Nathan looked around. Big John stood near the barn shooting him puzzled looks. No wonder. He didn't even know the guy had left. "He's worried about the hay getting wet," Nathan muttered.

"Yep, and he's going to take care of it. Right now I'm more concerned about you."

"Why? I'm fine." He turned toward the house but stopped. "Next week is Dad's birthday. You're invited to dinner."

"You going?"

Nathan nodded. He'd missed the celebration for the past two years. Time to quit being a self-absorbed ass.

"Good for you," Woody said quietly. "You taking Beth?"

"I asked her. Told her to bring Liberty."

"She turn you down? Is that why the long face?"

"She's thinking about it." Nathan shrugged, then eyed his friend. "You writing a gossip column for the *Gazette*?"

"Maybe. You got something juicy for me?"

Chuckling, Nathan shook his head. He stared up at the dark clouds coming from the north. Only a week ago he'd been studying the stars with Beth. "You think Liberty has a crush on me?"

Woody barked out a laugh. Then frowned. "Well, hells

bells, I think she just might. Wouldn't that be something? Here you being old enough to—"

"Yeah, I know." Nathan sighed. "Big John is right. Looks like rain, maybe even snow by tonight. Let's get the hay moved."

"Hold on there, son. I don't know what's got you all twisted up inside, but whatever it is…don't you let that gal go."

Nathan paused, though he wasn't about to get into a discussion about Beth. Not today. "I might not have a choice."

Woody's eyes narrowed. "Now, that's something I never expected to come out of your mouth. You're the most single-minded, bull-headed person I know. You want something, it's as good as got. So I reckon that means I was wrong. You mustn't want her so badly."

The old-timer jammed his hat back on his head and ambled toward the barn. Nathan knew damn well he hadn't heard the last of it. Woody liked to dispense words of "wisdom" whenever they popped into his head. He'd only made it a few yards before he turned and walked back to Nathan. Had to be a record, even for Woody.

"You been sitting on that pity pot so long I expect you must have a ring around your ass by now," Woody said, holding up a gnarled finger. "Get off, Nathan. Right now. It's past time."

Shocked, Nathan watched his friend turn on his heel and head back to the barn. People thought he was feeling sorry for himself? What complete bullshit.

AFTER PUTTING IT off for two days, on Monday Beth decided she'd have that talk with Liberty. Not just about going to the birthday dinner, but about her relationship with Nathan. No, he hadn't admitted that his feelings for her had changed, but that was because he was gun-shy after all he'd gone through with Anne. Beth wouldn't give him a pass forever, but she could for now.

Candace wasn't there when Beth got home from work, and shock of all shocks, Liberty was at the kitchen table doing homework. That alone justified another delay, except it wasn't fair to Nathan. He hadn't pushed, and in fact hadn't even mentioned it the few times they'd talked over the weekend, but she needed to give him an answer.

While she waited for Lib to finish her history paper, Beth made grilled-cheese sandwiches and heated a can of tomato soup for their dinner. Tomorrow she'd pick up stuff for salads at the Food Mart. Maybe she'd even put together some homemade soup.

Out of her peripheral vision she saw Lib close her book and the laptop Beth had given her. "Hey…do they still teach home-ec courses in high school?"

"What's that?"

"Guess that answers my question." Beth would've been surprised if the program still existed. She'd only wanted to start some conversation. "You want to learn how to cook?"

"From you?" Liberty sounded genuinely horrified.

"I'll have you know from the age of ten I did most of the cooking for your mom, Grandma and myself."

"Seriously? That's not very encouraging."

"Yeah." Beth laughed. "I can follow a recipe, though."

Liberty didn't look convinced, but she said, "You do make good grilled cheese."

"Thanks." With a rueful smile, Beth handed her the plate with her sandwich and a cup of soup. "Speaking of dinner, Nathan invited us to his folks' place next Wednesday," she said on her way back to the stove. "It's his dad's birthday and they're having a small get-together, mostly family. Woody will be there, too."

She'd kept her tone casual and purposely hadn't looked at Liberty. But when the silence lasted too long, she turned to check Lib's reaction.

Her niece was staring at her. "He asked both of us?"

Beth froze at Liberty's devastated expression. "I think he meant your mom, too."

"Yeah, right. I know you guys have been sneaking around. I'm not stupid."

Beth's heart sank. "What do you mean?" she asked weakly, feeling guilt heat her face.

Liberty stared at her. "Oh, my God. It's true." She let out a small gasp. "You've been seeing each other and lying. Those weekends away, you were with him…."

Too late Beth realized that Liberty hadn't known anything. She'd been fishing, and Beth had fallen for it. "Liberty, please…yes, Nathan and I are friends, but that doesn't change how either of us feels about you—"

"You're just like Candace." Liberty pushed away from the table, her chair screeching against the floor, her face red with anger. "You're both mean and selfish and take whatever you want. You don't care about me. She won't let me see my dad, and now you've stolen Nathan from me. I can't have anything for myself. Ever."

"Liberty, please try to calm down." Beth put a hand out to her, but Liberty jerked away and ran out of the kitchen. Seconds later her bedroom door slammed.

Beth felt as if the wind had been knocked out of her. Trying to take a deep breath made her lungs burn as if they were on fire. She smelled her grilled-cheese sandwich burning, turned off the stove and slid the frying pan off the red-hot coil. What the hell was she supposed to do now? Give Liberty time to cool off or plead to let her explain?

Oh, God, explain what? That her aunt was a liar. That Beth, knowing how it could affect Liberty, had continued to see Nathan. She had no excuse. She could apologize until she was blue in the face, but those were just empty words. When put to the test, she'd risked her relationship with Liberty and chosen Nathan. This time she couldn't even blame Candace.

To think Beth had been furious to learn of her sister's overnight disappearance last weekend while Beth was away. She was no better than Candace. No, she was worse, because Candace was clueless and Beth knew better. Yet she'd hurt Liberty anyway.

Queasy from guilt and the smell of burned bread, she sank onto a wobbly kitchen chair. A few weeks ago Beth had questioned Spike's motives and urged Liberty to evaluate the supposed friendship. Beth had asked her niece if she trusted her…asked if she believed Beth had her best interests at heart.

Liberty had looked so young and fragile when she'd met Beth's eyes and nodded. The memory pierced her heart like a stab to the chest. Feeling sick to her stomach, she bent to tuck her head between her knees. As soon as the nausea passed, she got to her feet. She couldn't let this ugliness between them fester overnight.

She knocked on Lib's door, prepared to bare her soul, beg for forgiveness, promise Liberty anything.

At first she didn't answer. Beth knocked again, and Lib screamed, "Go away."

"Please, Liberty," Beth pleaded. "Please talk to me."

In answer, Lib cranked her CD player to an earsplitting level.

Beth pressed her cheek to the door and closed her

eyes. "I love you, kiddo," she whispered, and then slowly straightened.

The short walk to the living room seemed to take a lifetime.

SUNLIGHT WAS SEEPING in between the curtains when Beth awoke. Startled, she glanced around the room, then at her phone lying on the cushion next to her. The last she'd checked, it had been 5:15 a.m. Apparently she'd fallen asleep sitting up on the couch sometime after that. Her neck and back were both stiff and her vision was blurry.

She picked up her cell, blinked and focused. Holy crap! How could it be 8:30 a.m. already? Forcing herself to her feet, she studied her phone. She had several missed calls...none from Candace, three from Nathan. After the blowup with Liberty, Beth had let his calls go to voice mail. No, it wasn't fair to ignore him, but she was incapable of speaking to him without making everything worse.

She checked Lib's room, not expecting to find her there. It was the usual mess, clothes in piles on the floor, the bed unmade—but at least it had been slept in—and the backpack she used for school was gone. Homeroom had just started, and Beth prayed Lib had caught the bus the way she always did.

The kitchen hadn't been touched since Beth had left the frying pan in the sink and dumped their dinner in the trash. Still, it bothered her that she hadn't heard the girl moving around. Of course, Liberty had probably gone into stealth mode, hoping to avoid another confrontation.

Stretching her neck and back, Beth glanced out the window. Candace wasn't home. Yeah, big surprise.

She needed a hot shower. But first she called Joe to tell him she was running late. Good thing she'd given him a key to the boardinghouse last week.

She made it into her closet-size room before it registered that her purse wasn't hanging from the doorknob where she'd left it. She searched the floor and behind the door. Her pulse slowed when she spotted the brown leather bag, except she never hung it on the door hook. She brought it down and looked inside. Her wallet was unsnapped. Even before she checked she knew her cash was gone. So was her debit card.

"Jesus, Liberty," she whispered, frozen with shock.

Forcing her feet to move, she raced to the kitchen and ripped the list of emergency numbers off the fridge. Her hand shaking, she called the school.

Liberty hadn't shown up for homeroom.

Not expecting her to answer, Beth tried Lib's cell anyway, and was sent to voice mail. She left a brief message, then tried calling Candace with no luck. Her bedroom door was closed, which probably meant nothing. Driven by a funny feeling, Beth knocked once then opened it.

Something was off. The room was too neat. No dirty clothes littered the stained carpet, and the dresser wasn't covered with trays of makeup. The room seemed…empty. On the nightstand, tucked under the red lava lamp, was an envelope. Her stomach coiling into a knot, Beth walked over and picked it up. The power company's return address had been crossed off, and in Candace's handwriting, Beth's name was scrawled across the used envelope.

With shaking fingers, she opened it up and read the short message.

It's better for everyone if I'm out of the picture. Besides, you always wanted to have Liberty to yourself. Now you've got her. No hard feelings. This is better for her. Tell her goodbye for me and not to worry. I found me a real good guy this time.

17

NATHAN HAD JUST pulled up in front of the boardinghouse when his cell buzzed. Relief rolled through him when he saw it was Beth. They hadn't spoken at the appointed hour last night because she hadn't answered his calls. And now her truck wasn't parked in its usual spot. Something was wrong.

"Beth? Where are you?"

"Nathan…thank God." She sounded out of breath. "By any chance have you seen Liberty? Is she at the ranch?"

"No. Wouldn't she be in school?"

"Yes, she should be." Her voice broke. "We had an argument last night and now she's missing. She won't answer her cell."

"She'll show up," he said calmly. "Every kid runs away at some point. Hell, she's probably blowing off steam with a spray can." Not a pleasant thought. Maybe he should've left that out.

"I'm afraid it's more serious than that. Is it possible she's there with Woody and you just haven't seen her?" She paused, and he heard her sniff. "She might be avoiding you, too."

"I'll check with him. Where are you?"

"At home, but I'm getting ready to go look for her."

"Stay put. I'm in town. I'll pick you up in ten minutes."

"No," she said, her voice shrill with panic. "You can't go with me. You'll only make things worse. She knows about us, Nathan. She tricked me into admitting it. I feel so stupid. I'm a liar and a hypocrite and I—I have to go."

"Wait." Fear gripped him. "You're too upset to drive. Please, trust me."

The endless silence singed his nerve endings. Flashing back to that night he'd received the call about Anne's accident, he started to sweat. At the time he'd gone through shock, denial, anger in a matter of minutes. Now all he felt was utter terror.

"Beth, don't do this." He turned the truck around toward her place. Christ, if anything happened to her...

"I'll wait," she said evenly. "Don't speed. I'll be here when you get here."

Their roles had reversed. She'd obviously heard his panic and was trying to calm him down. That was the thing, she understood him. It didn't seem possible given their short acquaintance, but that was the truth. Last night he'd finally admitted to himself that he'd fallen in love with her. He just hadn't figured out if he should tell her. Guess now wasn't the time.

BETH WAS SITTING in her truck when Nathan arrived. She'd been taking long, deep breaths, trying to at least appear calm. Inside she was a wreck. She understood why he'd be worried. He was thinking about Anne, of course, and while Beth didn't want to put him through the hell of waiting and fearing the worst, she couldn't take him with her.

He parked directly in front of her. Much as it pissed

her off that he'd deliberately hemmed her in, she forced herself not to react when he got out and opened her door.

"I'll drive," he said. "We'll take my truck."

"I have to do this alone."

"Don't be foolish, Beth. You're in no condition to drive."

"Nathan, this is my fault and my responsibility, not yours. I appreciate that you want to help—"

"I don't give a damn about any of that...." He took a deep shuddering breath. "Look at you...you're as white as a sheet. Your hands are shaking. How much good will you be to Liberty if you wrap yourself around a pole?"

"You don't look so hot yourself."

Briefly closing his eyes, he passed a hand over his face. "I needed to know you were okay," he said. "I'm fine now. Let's do this together."

She wished she could ease the lines of tension at the corners of his eyes, tension she had caused. But she couldn't even stop her own hands from shaking. "You can drive, but we'll take my truck. Once we find her, you can't get out, no matter what. Are we clear?"

"Whatever you say." He stepped back to let her out. "But consider that if she spots you first she might hide. This color blue you can see a mile away."

Beth saw his point. Without another word, she climbed into his black truck. When had her life spun so out of control? It seemed things had started to unravel the moment she'd decided to move to Blackfoot Falls—or maybe when she'd met Nathan. She couldn't think straight, had no idea where to go or who else to call....

"Let's go to the high school. Spike is there, I checked. He's in class, so his phone is turned off, but he might know something." She stared at her cell, then speed dialed Liberty. Of course, no answer.

"Call Marge at the diner. Even if she hasn't seen Liberty, she can spread the word."

"I already called while I was waiting for you. I talked to pretty much everyone in town. Someone told me Lib was on the bus. She took off after the kids were dropped off at school."

"I alerted Woody. He's got guys combing the barns and sheds. If he doesn't find her, he'll take Craig with him and drive to town. They might get lucky and see her walking."

"Thank you," she murmured softly. "God, I'm so sorry I'm interrupting everyone's life."

Nathan reached over and squeezed her cold hand. His warm, comforting touch brought tears to her eyes. Tears she couldn't afford to indulge. She jerked her hand away and turned to stare out her window until the waterworks subsided.

"I can't believe how badly I messed up," she whispered. "I was sitting on the deck of a ship sailing to Italy when I got Liberty's text. It was the Fourth of July and we passed an American destroyer with flags strung from bow to stern. For the first time since leaving home, I felt homesick. I mean, really, deep-down homesick." She snorted. "Not for the trailer park. God, I hated that place. I kept waiting for someone to tow that rickety old trailer out from under us. It happened to my friend three trailers over. We never saw each other again." She glanced sheepishly at Nathan, wishing she hadn't volunteered so much.

He kept his eyes on the road, no judgment in his expression. "So Liberty asked you to move back?"

"She sounded so desperate. I knew my sister well and I knew Lib hadn't been exaggerating. Then Candace called." Beth didn't need to go into that. "I made up my mind right then. I was going to come home and fix everything. Yeah, great job."

"Yep, you've done a helluva job. What, you've been here four, five months? Were you expecting a miracle?"

Beth sighed and turned back to the window. He didn't get it. He had a functional family and no kids. She didn't expect him to understand.

Neither of them spoke the rest of the drive. He stayed in the truck while she went to the principal's office for permission to talk to Spike. She'd met him twice before, and while she couldn't stand the belligerent little punk, he'd been useful.

By the time she ran back to the truck, Nathan had it in gear. "I think she's trying to catch a bus," Beth said. "Do you know Carterville?"

"Well, yeah, it's about an hour east." He'd started driving the second she closed the door. "The bus station is small. Call and give them her description."

It seemed like the connection took forever, and then she got an answering machine and had to listen to a list of schedules. At the end, her only option was to leave a message. "Dammit."

"They share the building with a pawnshop. Call them."

She gave the station another try and someone picked up. Liberty had boarded a bus that had left fifteen minutes earlier. Beth had already figured out her niece would try to see her father. And knowing what Beth had recently learned from Candace, she felt sick about it. At any cost, she had to stop Lib before she got to the prison.

"There she is," Nathan said, nodding toward the tiny convenience store. Lib had just exited with a can of soda and was heading back to the bus. "Where should I park?"

"Close. I may need you."

He shot her a puzzled look but only nodded.

It had been his idea to cut her off at the next stop. Beth was so strung out she probably would've had the bus company's dispatcher call the driver, and that would have made things infinitely worse. Maybe she should've told him about Candace's note, but she was still trying to figure out what to say to Liberty.

He pulled into the parking spot closest to the bus and she climbed out of the truck. Luckily, Liberty was busy chatting with a young mother and her toddler and didn't see Beth approach.

"Hey, kiddo."

Liberty spun around, regarded her with wide-eyed shock that slid into a glare. "What are you doing here?"

"I came to take you home," Beth said in a low calm voice.

"No. I'm not ever going back there. And you can't make me."

"Actually, I can."

Liberty's defiant expression slipped for a moment, then resurged as she stared past Beth. "Is that why you brought him? So you can force me?"

Beth didn't bother looking. She knew Nathan was standing close behind her, though she hadn't meant for him to get out of the truck unless she signaled for him. "No one is going to force you," Beth said calmly, aware of the interested onlookers. "But if it becomes necessary I'll notify the sheriff and let him handle returning you to Blackfoot Falls. You are a minor."

Liberty reared back as if she'd been slapped. "Bullshit. I'm going to see my dad, and he won't let you."

"Nice language." Beth glanced at the toddler.

The girl turned red and mumbled an apology to the mother. "Aunt Beth, please, I know you don't agree with

Candace. You think I should be able to visit my dad. Let me see him. Please."

She cleared her throat, hoping she had the strength to do this. Nathan touched her shoulder and she looked at him.

He drew her several feet back and spoke low in her ear. "I can drive you both to the prison. We're only a few hours away."

"No." Damn him. This was already hard enough. "Thank you." She turned back to Liberty and saw quite clearly that she'd heard Nathan. Beth straightened her spine. "The answer is still no.... You stole money from my purse, Liberty. Now, get in the truck."

Shame tamed her anger. "I was going to pay you back."

The bus driver walked out of the store and announced everyone had to board.

Beth refused to break eye contact. "Are you coming, or should I call the sheriff?"

Lib glared back. "I hate you," she said, and shouldered past her. "You're just like Candace."

The return trip to Blackfoot Falls was silent and tense. Liberty used her earbuds to listen to her iPod. And though she had the volume loud enough to deafen a whole city, Beth didn't dare have a conversation with Nathan. It was clear he was wondering why she'd refused to let Lib visit her father. Beth had told him she disagreed with Candace and thought Lib should be allowed to see him. What he didn't know was that, for once in her life, Candace had done the right thing, the kind thing for her daughter.

Ray, the stupid prick, didn't want to see Liberty. He'd suddenly decided she wasn't his kid and threatened to tell her just that, then request a paternity test if he was forced to see her. Probably worried he'd be hit up for child support once he was out of prison. Candace had taken it on the chin rather than devastate Liberty. Beth would've had a new respect for her sister if she hadn't turned around and done something equally selfish.

Nathan pulled into the driveway. Liberty jumped out and stormed into the house. Beth briefly wondered if she should board her bedroom window shut. She wasn't looking forward to telling the girl about Candace, and God only knew how she'd react.

"Thank you," she said, turning to Nathan. Alarmed when she saw he'd started to open his door, she laid a hand on his arm. "You were right. I was in no condition to drive and you were terrific. I'm sorry about Liberty's behavior."

He let go of the door handle and settled back, the sudden sadness in his face making her want to cry. Did he know this was it for them? He had to suspect. "Maybe it would help if I came in and talked to her."

She shook her head. "It's about to get worse, I think," she said, and regretted the worry she'd put in his eyes. "Maybe not. What do I know about teenage girls these days?"

He cupped a hand around the back of her neck, knowing exactly where to rub away the tension. Except this time she didn't think it would work. "I'm going to ask you something and I don't want you to say no right off. I'd like you to think about it." He waited for her to nod, so she did, though she couldn't imagine there was a magic solution for them. "I want you to come stay at the Lucky 7. For however long you want. Let your sister and Liberty work things out. You need to destress."

Beth just stared at him. Was he out of his mind?

"Think about it. Liberty knows, so we aren't hiding from her anymore. In a few days she'll get over it, and she's welcome to come over as much as she wants. She loves working with the horses—"

"Nathan. Stop. I can't." She swallowed. "Candace is gone. She left me a note. Liberty is solely my responsibility now."

He looked stunned. She knew the feeling. Why hadn't she seen this coming?

"Well, okay." He stared at the house. Ran a hand through his hair. "Then you bring Liberty. You know I have plenty of room. Woody will keep her busy when she's not in school—"

Beth smiled. "You brave, stupid man. She's a teenager. I'm guessing she'll hate us for more than a few days." She meant it. He was brave. He hadn't planned on adding a willful niece to his invitation, but he was trying to smooth the rough edges, and she admired him for that.

She admired him for so many things. He was a good man. This was her fault. Even if he didn't understand how damaging it was to send the wrong message to Liberty. This was all Beth's fault. And she would probably spend part of her life regretting having ruined things for them. She'd known better all along. Her mission had always been to protect Liberty. Now it was more important than ever that she step up. Repair the damage she'd done by sneaking around—and for what? Sex? Beth knew better. She should've kept them out of the bedroom.

"I have to go," she said, her heart breaking into a hundred pieces.

Nathan looked shell-shocked. "Will you call?"

"Sure," she said, and kissed him on the cheek.

A WEEK LATER Beth still hadn't called. Frankly, Nathan hadn't expected her to. He supposed he could've made the effort himself, but he'd been too steamed. While he hadn't expected a parade down Main Street for helping her find Liberty, he sure as hell hadn't deserved to be cut off. He wasn't blaming her for making Liberty her priority, but did that mean they were supposed to stay away from each other forever? Pretend that they hadn't gone and fallen in love?

Yeah, he was real clear on how he felt about her. And dammit, he was pretty sure she was feeling it, too. But knowing her, she was too wrapped in guilt to cut herself a break.

Even if the truth hadn't made it past his thick skull, he had Woody and Clint reminding him. They were like two old women, nagging him to go see Beth and irritating him at every turn. He wasn't all that surprised about Woody sticking his nose where it didn't belong, but Clint shocked him. Fine time for Nathan to be easing his way back into the family. Maybe he should send the two busybodies to go work on Beth. It seemed she could use the convincing.

Sitting in his office, Nathan stared at the spreadsheets on his computer screen. He'd been trying to go over the books for two hours and hadn't gotten a damn thing done. Of course, he kept thinking about Beth. Hearing about her childhood fear of getting their trailer towed away had really gotten to him. It had struck too close to home. His own family had almost lost Whispering Pines because of financial problems. Worrying that you could lose your home wasn't something a person got over easily.

No question Beth wanted to protect Liberty. But he wondered how much of her desperation had to do with feeling like that helpless little girl who'd never seen her friend again.

And what about him? What role had his fear played in driving him to succeed? He'd sworn up and down he'd be a better businessman than his father. And he'd accomplished that goal. But had his single-minded focus cost him his marriage? His dad was probably the best husband and father Nathan knew. In that arena, Nathan had failed miserably.

Jesus, he couldn't seem to turn off his brain.

He rubbed his tired eyes. Life sure had some funny twists and turns. Here he'd half expected the day would come when Beth tired of Blackfoot Falls and returned to her old job. Wouldn't happen. She was dedicated to saving Liberty. That was the thing that could keep them apart. Maybe she'd figured out he'd end up disappointing the both of them.

Weary and disgusted, he closed the spreadsheet. No use sitting and staring. His gaze swept the bookcase on the back wall and caught on the bookends Anne had given him for his birthday. They were silly. Two bronze figures—he didn't know why he hadn't gotten rid of them. God, Anne and Beth were so different. Going to all those estate sales had shown him Beth's taste. More sentimental than he'd imagined, but not silly. Huh.

He paused before he turned off his computer. Beth wasn't Anne, and he wasn't the same young firebrand who'd married Anne. So he'd failed once at a relationship. Did that mean he had to give up on something even better? Or did he want to fight for Beth? Prove that they were meant for each other?

BETH LOOKED UP and smiled when Liberty entered the office. "Hey you, how was school?"

Liberty shrugged as she dumped her backpack on the spare chair before grabbing a soda. "Melissa asked me to go have lunch at the diner. Can I go?"

Beth looked at the time and wanted to weep. Only

12:30 p.m.? She'd forgotten that school got out early today. The morning had dragged by, just like every other morning for the past ten days. Dammit, she missed Nathan.

She knew it was too soon for Lib to have gotten over the betrayals in her life. Bad enough her aunt had "stolen" her crush, but Candace had broken her heart. Beth just hoped it could be mended in time.

At least Lib was talking to her again. They'd even had a few good heart-to-heart discussions, and Beth was grateful for the new closeness between them. Missing Nathan so desperately wasn't helping, though.

Lib was staring at her.

Beth blinked. Lunch. They'd been talking about lunch.

"Okay, look. I know you want to call him. So call him. I don't care. Just, can I go with Melissa or not?"

Beth tried to swallow. This was the first time Liberty had brought up Nathan. And she seemed so calm. "You mean that?"

"That I want to go to lunch? Yeah."

"Don't be like that. We promised, no more lies."

"I wasn't lying. I was trying to avoid this conversation. Yes. I meant it. I don't care. Okay?"

Beth jumped to her feet.

Liberty eyed her warily. "Oh, man, you're going to hug me, aren't you?"

"Yes, I am. Get over it." Beth threw her arms around Liberty and almost lifted her off the chair. "No one is more important than you. Do you hear me?"

"Well, yeah, you're yelling in my ear."

Beth laughed. "No one can ever take your place in my heart. No one. I will never abandon you, kiddo. Never. I love you." She leaned back. "That doesn't mean I won't have relationships with other people," she said gently.

"But you never have to feel threatened or be afraid that you'll be replaced."

They heard a knock and turned toward the door.

Liberty blushed and lowered her head.

"Hey, Nathan," Beth said casually, even though her pulse was stuck on overdrive. "We were just talking about you. Is Woody here, too?"

"Nope." He glanced cautiously at Lib, then back to Beth. "He's at the ranch. Doesn't school let out later?"

Beth winked at Liberty, who didn't seem so embarrassed anymore. "She got time off for good behavior."

She grinned at Liberty's snort.

"I gotta meet my friend for lunch," Lib said, but she waited until she got Beth's nod. Then she made a move for the door.

"Wait," Nathan said. "I wanted to ask you both something. Thanksgiving is next week and I'd like you to go with me to my folks' house. Think it over. No pressure."

Beth couldn't have been more surprised if he'd walked in without a shirt. Of course, her mind would have to go *there*. For God's sake.

Lib seemed even more stunned. She stared at Nathan, looking totally confused.

"There'll be plenty of pumpkin pie," he said, his voice gentle. "And horses. Lots of horses."

The blush returned, but it must have been too much to expect her to respond. Liberty left. At least she didn't slam the door.

Beth took a deep breath before meeting Nathan's eyes. He'd been studying her.

"How've you been?" he asked.

"Busy. You know, with Liberty, the renovation. You?"

"Yep, I've been busy, too."

"I imagine the Arabians are taking up a lot of your time."

"Somewhat. Though Clint's been working with me."

"Really?" She didn't understand why that pleased her so much. "I'm glad."

"Look," he said, motioning with his chin toward the door. "I didn't expect Liberty to be here. But when she didn't throw any daggers at me, I figured it was okay to bring up Thanksgiving."

Beth nodded. "Sure. As you saw, she's okay. We've been doing a lot together and working through some stuff. She's handling things better than I'd expected, to be honest." She hated being so nervous. She wished she'd at least put on some makeup, but that was nothing. Feeling jumpy with him? To quote Lib, that sucked. "It's gonna take some time, though."

"If the nonmoody days outnumber the I-hate-you-and-everybody-on-the-planet ones, you're in good shape."

"What?" Beth smiled. "Since when are you an expert?"

"I've been doing a lot of reading this past week. Mostly online, but I bought a few books, too. About teenagers, particularly ones who've suffered troubled childhoods." His solemn expression told her he wasn't joking. When he took her hand, she was too stunned to object. "I've learned a lot. You were right about sending wrong messages. Poor kid's been getting those for years. But Liberty also needs to see what a healthy relationship looks like, what it means to be equal partners who love and respect each other. Take us, for instance."

"Um…" She stared into his unwavering gaze, her heart pounding wildly as he drew her closer.

"I love you, Beth. I should've told you before now. Or maybe you're wishing I'd kept my feelings to myself.

Lord knows it wouldn't be my first mistake." His mouth curved in a crooked smile she'd never seen before. "I'd really appreciate it if you'd say something about now."

"Wait. Back up." She swallowed. "Did you say you love me?"

Nathan groaned, looking as nervous as she'd felt before she'd gone numb. "I swore to myself I wouldn't bring this up now. Or make any assumptions, but I think you feel the same way. Tell me I'm not wrong, Beth. Tell me you love me, too." He took a deep breath. "And if you can't, I'll wait."

She pulled him down into a kiss. Then she rocked back to look into his eyes, troubled to find fear and uncertainty.

"I'm not fooling myself," he said. "We'll have plenty of bumps in the road with Liberty. She won't lose her fears and resentment overnight, but together we can give her a good life. We just have to be firm and consistent, and she'll come around."

"Shut up."

"What?" A faint smile tugged at his mouth.

"Do you want to hear me say it or not?" How could she not love this wonderful, caring man? He didn't just want her, he was willing to take on Liberty, as well.

Nathan smiled. "Say it."

"I love you, Nathan Landers. With all my heart."

He pulled her into his arms. "I took some wrong turns the first time around, but I'm very clear on what kind of man I want to be. I'll work hard to never disappoint you."

Beth knew tears were close. "You won't have to work hard at all." She kissed him again. "I know exactly who you are. That's the reason I love you."

No, she didn't need a man to make her happy, but she did want Nathan. For the two months they'd been together, she'd felt content and safe, even when life continued to dish out challenges.

"Bethany, will you marry me?" He touched her cheek. "Not for Liberty's sake. For mine."

"Yes," she whispered, and let the happy tears fall.

* * * * *

COMING NEXT MONTH FROM

Available September 16, 2014

#815 WICKED NIGHTS
Uniformly Hot!
by Anne Marsh
When local bad boy SEAL Cal Brennan threatens to put
Piper Clark's dive shop out of business, she'll do anything to
take him down a notch. Including proposing a sexy bet where
the loser takes orders from the winner for one night...in bed.

#816 SOME LIKE IT HOTTER
by Isabel Sharpe
California free-spirit Eva and her Manhattan sophisticate twin
sister agree to swap coasts and coffee shops—to perk things
up. When busy exec Ames Bradford makes stopping by a
nightly habit, Eva's soon brewing it up hot and satisfying!

#817 CLOSE UP
From Every Angle
by Erin McCarthy
Kristine Zimmerman is finally divorcing the man she left years
ago. Sean Maddock is even hotter now but there's nothing left
between them, right? Then he proposes a deliciously sinful
weekend for old times' sake...and she can't think of a single
reason to refuse.

#818 TRIPLE THREAT
The Art of Seduction
by Regina Kyle
Playwright Holly Ryan's Broadway dream may come true with
the help of sexy blockbuster star—and former high school
crush—Nick Damone. The heat and intensity between them
might set the stage on fire!

REQUEST YOUR FREE BOOKS!
2 FREE NOVELS PLUS 2 FREE GIFTS!

red-hot reads!

YES! Please send me 2 FREE Harlequin® Blaze™ novels and my 2 FREE gifts (gifts are worth about $10). After receiving them, if I don't wish to receive any more books, I can return the shipping statement marked "cancel." If I don't cancel, I will receive 4 brand-new novels every month and be billed just $4.74 book in the U.S. or $4.96 per book in Canada. That's a savings of at least 14% off the cover price. It's quite a bargain. Shipping and handling is just 50¢ per book in the U.S. and 75¢ per book in Canada.* I understand that accepting the 2 free books and gifts places me under no obligation to buy anything. I can always return a shipment and cancel at any time. Even if I never buy another book, the two free books and gifts are mine to keep forever.

150/350 HDN F4WC

Name	(PLEASE PRINT)

Address	Apt. #

City	State/Prov.	Zip/Postal Code

Signature (if under 18, a parent or guardian must sign)

Mail to the Harlequin® Reader Service:
IN U.S.A.: P.O. Box 1867, Buffalo, NY 14240-1867
IN CANADA: P.O. Box 609, Fort Erie, Ontario L2A 5X3

Want to try two free books from another line?
Call 1-800-873-8635 or visit www.ReaderService.com.

* Terms and prices subject to change without notice. Prices do not include applicable taxes. Sales tax applicable in N.Y. Canadian residents will be charged applicable taxes. Offer not valid in Quebec. This offer is limited to one order per household. Not valid for current subscribers to Harlequin Blaze books. All orders subject to credit approval. Credit or debit balances in a customer's account(s) may be offset by any other outstanding balance owed by or to the customer. Please allow 4 to 6 weeks for delivery. Offer available while quantities last.

Your Privacy—The Harlequin® Reader Service is committed to protecting your privacy. Our Privacy Policy is available online at www.ReaderService.com or upon request from the Harlequin Reader Service.

We make a portion of our mailing list available to reputable third parties that offer products we believe may interest you. If you prefer that we not exchange your name with third parties, or if you wish to clarify or modify your communication preferences, please visit us at www.ReaderService.com/consumerschoice or write to us at Harlequin Reader Service Preference Service, P.O. Box 9062, Buffalo, NY 14269. Include your complete name and address.

HB13R2

SPECIAL EXCERPT FROM

HARLEQUIN®

Blaze®

Read on for an excerpt from

Wicked Nights

by New York Times *bestselling author Anne Marsh.*

Piper was naked.

Okay, so she wasn't totally naked, but a man could dream.

Somehow, he'd timed his arrival at her slip for the precise moment she grabbed the zipper running up the back of her wet suit. Undeterred by his presence—because surely she'd heard him snap her name—she pulled, the neoprene suit parting slow and steady beneath her touch.

Hello.

Each new inch of sun-kissed skin she revealed made certain parts of him spring to life.

Even as he reminded himself that she'd spent most of their early days trying to either torment or kill him, however, his eyes were busy. Piper's arms were spectacular, strong and toned from hour after hour of pulling herself through the water and then back up into the boat. Now she was looking sexier than any stripper, uncovering skin that was a rich golden brown from time outdoors. The way she'd braided her water-slicked hair in a severe plait only drew his attention to the deceptively vulnerable curve of her neck.

But this was *Piper*.

So dragging his tongue over her skin and tasting all the

places where she was still damp from her dive should have been the *last* thing on his mind. He'd read her the riot act about her careless driving and say his piece about tomorrow's business meeting. Then he'd go his way and she'd go hers.

The wet suit hit her waist.

Neither short nor tall, Piper had medium-brown hair, brown eyes and a slim build. Those cut-and-dried facts didn't begin to do the woman in front of him justice, however. They certainly didn't begin to explain why he unexpectedly found her so appealing or why he wanted to wrap an arm around her and take her down to the deck for a kiss. Or seven. He didn't like Piper. He never had. She'd also made it plenty clear that he irritated her on a regular basis.

So why was he staring at her like a drowning man?

And…score another point for Piper. Like many divers, she hadn't bothered with a bikini top beneath the three-millimeter suit. His kiss quote rocketed up to double digits.

"Piper." His voice sounded hoarse to his own ears. *Focus.*

She jumped, her head swinging around toward him. "If it isn't my favorite SEAL."

**Pick up WICKED NIGHTS
by *New York Times* bestselling author
Anne Marsh.**

**Available October 2014 wherever
you buy books and ebooks.**

The EX Factor!

Kristine Zimmerman is finally divorcing the man she left years ago. Sean Maddock is even hotter now, but there's nothing left between them, right? Then he proposes a deliciously sinful weekend for old times' sake...and she can't think of a single reason to refuse!

From the reader-favorite

***From Every Angle* trilogy,**

Close Up

by *Erin McCarthy*

Available October 2014 wherever you buy Harlequin Blaze books.

And don't miss

Double Exposure,

the first in the

***From Every Angle* trilogy, already available!**

HARLEQUIN®

Blaze®

Red-Hot Reads

www.Harlequin.com